The NOBLE SAVAGE

:

Also by Nora M. Barraford

The Strawman Burns, 1971
The Secular Supernatural, 1986
Coat Color in Cats, 1986
Tittle Tattle, 2006
Barraford-Jenne, A Multilineal Genealogy, 1986

Also by Andrew E. Barraford

The Golden Sphere, 1990
The Drop, 2002
The American Manifesto, 2003

(For her books, see Nora's website: www.norabarrford.com)

The NOBLE SAVAGE

& Other Pertinent Discussions

Nora Barraford

iUniverse, Inc.

New York   Bloomington

The Noble Savage

& Other Pertinent Discussions

iUniverse books may be ordered through booksellers or by contacting:

iUniverse
1663 Liberty Drive
Bloomington, IN 47403
www.iuniverse.com
1-800-Authors (1-800-288-4677)

ISBN: 978-0-595-42776-5 (pbk)
ISBN: 978-0-595-71125-3 (cloth)
ISBN: 978-0-595-87107-0 (ebk)

Printed in the United States of America

iUniverse rev. date: 12/24/2008

Dedication

This book, The Noble Savage, is dedicated on November 2, 2005 to the most wonderful parents anyone ever had: Andrew Joseph MacDonnell I and Eva May (Law) MacDonnell, his wife. They taught me I could do anything I wanted as long as I didn't hurt others. They taught me never to be ashamed of my own endeavors, even if they were not as outstanding as those of George Washington Carver or Leonardo da Vinci. As my mother once said, when I hung one of my own paintings on the wall, I might not have a da Vinci, but I didn't have somebody else's copy on that wall: I had an original "Nora".

All the stories in this book are based on the quirky humor of my father, Andrew Joseph MacDonnell I, who could not resist embellishing any story he told with his Irish humor.

Nora Mary (MacDonnell) Barraford,

BA, AM, MFA, Ph.D.

Professor Emeritus, Worcester State College,

Worcester, MA

Contents

Prologue

Although some anecdotal stories within the chapters date back to the 1920's, the original Noble Savage articles were written between 1990 and 2003. None were published until some public event, like that of the Japanese calling the American workers lazy, caused me to publish one called "On Laziness", which was an apt rebuttal to the remark. Remembering my Dad and what he would say inspired me to write another. Dad was able to find something funny or quixotic in everything.

He was a great lover of nature, especially birds. He called himself a little brother of St. Francis, because the wild creatures also loved him. When he sat in the backyard to rest after mowing the lawn or doing some other garden work, the birds would fly down and cover him from head to toe, rooting in his hair and pockets for the birdseed he hid there for them. They would cuddle under his hands or under his chin and hair to sleep for a time until he sat up. It may be hard for most people to understand, but there have been "bird-speakers" in every human race for countless centuries. My father was one of them.

Even as a boy, he had this talent. Once when he was a twelve year old, roaming in his father's mountainous Irish meadows, he found a wounded young crow. He carried it home, tended it and taught it to speak. It would not leave him when it could fly again, but always stayed close to him, sitting on his shoulder at meals or flying after him when he walked about. Sometimes it would pick something up and bring it to him or carry it away to a secret cache if he refused it—or ate it himself if it was a worm or bug. (The crow is a small type of raven, you know. European and Hindu ravens, "Rooks" or

"Rocs", are huge. They can pick up a hen, a cat, a baby lamb or even a very small child. Remember Aladdin?)

Dad kept the crow until it died of old age, then he stuffed it and carried it with him wherever he went (until mother buried the poor bird's decaying carcass somewhere where dad could not find its rotting remnants.)

Wherever we went, he kept birds, Algerian doves, canaries, pigeons, falcons. He even trained falcons for falconers. He used wild birds whenever he could get them, because, he said, they were easier to train and better hunters after training.

"Falcons are very smart," he would say, "They soon know which side their bread is buttered on. In the wild, they may not always find fresh meat. Hunting for a falconer they know that even if they do not always make a successful kill, when they return to their falconer's wrist, they will always have fresh meat waiting for them."

Of course, my father would ask me to remind you that he was not alone in his devotion to birds and other creatures of the world. The Indians not only had the sacred eagle, they also had the sacred white buffalo, with which their shaman took council. The Egyptians worshipped creatures from the cat to the golden beetle. The crow and the Rook (or Roc) were enfabled in both Egypt and India. Other Indo-Europeans, worshipped the bull god Al (Allah), or El. In the past, speaking with the animals was akin to speaking with a God, but Andrew Joseph MacDonnell was a down-to-earth man of the animals and people, when they acted as civilized as the animals he knew.

Finally, when I decided to collect these Noble Savage articles and turn them into a book, they seemed to jolt each other. Cement of some kind was needed to turn them into a cohesive whole. That was when my own tyrannical editor, one of my much loved sons, Andrew E. Barraford, came to my rescue with the additional sealing wax chapters to connect the articles into a story of which my father, the original Noble Savage, would heartily approve—as do I.

But now, let us meet the Noble Savage himself and put our questions to him.

Fleeing or Pursuing?

"What do you want?" No matter how harshly the editor stated it, I marveled at how succinctly he summed up the ultimate human question.

Every one of us is searching for something; the problem is we do not know what we are searching for, since in most cases we do not know what we want. Ostensibly, as a reporter, I was searching for a living human example of the good old days before man's civilized institutions had destroyed this hypothetical person's moral fiber, his feelings of compassion, and his duty towards those less fortunate than himself. I would like to say I was doing this for some grand, altruistic motive, but underneath the verbal graffiti, I just wanted to go somewhere other than where I was, in order to see that which otherwise I could not see, hoping that this change of perception would provide me a glimpse over the elusive horizon I was searching for.

Giving me a fierce scowl, the editor affixed me with his black eyes, framed in heavy black rimmed glasses, as I waited for the photographer that I had dragged in with me to settle down with his paraphernalia behind me.

"Perky and I would like to talk to you," I ignored the editor's brusque exterior, pointing my thumb like a hitchhiker at the shivering, red-headed mass of humanity behind me. Tall and lanky, Perky shifted from foot to foot, nervously, while shuffling his large camera with a humungous lens from arm to arm. When I had alluded to him, Perky's bright blue eyes bugged out and unbeknownst to me, Perky began shaking his head vigorously behind me.

"I don't have the time for this," the editor gruffly dismissed me, readjusting his black-rimmed glasses, and looking back at his papers as if I were a fly that had inadvertently buzzed into the room.

1

Getting what I wanted out of my editor was an art, which I worked at. Packing on a considerable amount of weight, probably from living in his seat perusing words for 20 years, the editor jostled his papers to make himself look busy, but his job was to watch everyone and make sure that *they* were busy. I had studied my editor more assiduously than the subjects whom I wrote about, and I recognized that he was hoping that I would simply go away.

"I have a proposal, Ed," I have always chuckled at the idea of an editor whose name was Ed. Ed, the editor, reminded me of a children's book character like Charlie the Choo-Choo train. "I want you to send me to South America."

No matter how painful this was going to be for my editor, the project that I was proposing would take me on my desired sabbatical to somewhere, but was I fleeing disillusionment or pursuing happiness? Both were intertwined and inseparable and depended in the end on what I really wanted.

"Argh!" Ed grunted, pushing himself back from his desk while rolling his eyes in disbelief in one short, but rather athletic movement, considering his weight.

"You're the one that has been moaning around the office about wanting anthropology or archaeology articles!" I accused. Ever since a television show, *Anthropology Today*, had become extremely popular, Ed had been stalking everyone in the office, asking for anthropology or archaeology articles like a hungry dog, repeatedly saying "give me a bone." I took the offensive, knowing that the strength of this interest would make or break my case. "I am giving you that bone you wanted."

"You think this will come up with a hot anthropology article?" The editor slyly looked at me and then directed his stare out the window, as if afraid that if I could look into his eyes, I could see his hidden eagerness blooming.

"Exactly," I fed Ed what he wanted to hear. "Imagine a series of articles on a primitive dweller of South America, who has often been referred to as the Noble Savage."

"How much is this going to cost?" Ed groaned.

"Don't you want to hear more about the Noble Savage?" I asked.

"How much?" Ed insisted.

"A couple of months of pay for two, transportation and expenses," I told him matter-of-factly.

"ARGH!" Ed shouted and then began to gnash his teeth and beat his chest. "That much money? How do you think I can afford that?"

Watching a small round man become overwrought would have been a very disturbing scene, if I had NOT seen it before and planned for it.

"How about this," I suggested furtively. "You can hold off on my salary, but you have to pay for Perky and the expenses. That should help your budget, but I get double the payback, if the series is syndicated."

The editor immediately stopped slavering, wiped the drool off his chin and began jotting down numerical notes on a partially smudged paper napkin left over from breakfast.

"And Perky, too?"

"No, Perky has to be paid," I clarified for him. Perky was short for Cecil Anstruther Perkins. (He won't answer to Cecil. Can't imagine why? Can you? And he says Anstruther is too antsy, even though he is a little antsy by nature.) A college boy, he was the quivering photographer that I had dragged into the room with me. Previously, he had worked for me during the summer breaks between terms, but, due to finances, he needed to take this semester off and work full-time. "He must make his school loan payments."

"I don't need to go," Perky stoked his courage and spoke up. The biggest source of his reluctance, not to mention his biggest personal flaw, was that he is a bon vivant; this journey would put a terrible crimp in his social plans, but his fear of the editor was profound, not to mention that his girlfriends' plans were getting a little elaborate lately, making him somewhat nervous.

"We need the photos," I responded dryly, and was surprised to see Ed nodding his head grimly in agreement.

Perky pondered his anguished dilemma. Between his fear of his editor, his girlfriends with delusions of matrimony and the fact that jobs were scarce, backing out of this adventure was not a viable option, although Perky really wished he had one.

"I don't pay salary, while you are in transit." Ed declared, ignoring Perky and breaking the short silence.

"That's not a problem," I agreed, thinking that losing a day of pay while I am on a plane was not a big issue.

"It might work," he muttered. "You would have to keep to an allowance of five dollar meals, two times a day."

It was my turn to roll my eyes.

"I'll survive," I agreed, thinking fast food is my friend.

"That's five dollars a meal for both of you!" Ed clarified.

"I know I need to go on a diet, but this is ridiculous!" I realized that I had agreed too quickly. Ed would buy into anything, as long as there was give and take; so when I gave in too readily, this was like a red flag to Ed that I would take less. We dickered on this subject for about half an hour, before Ed and I agreed on four dollars a day per person.

"What about this Noble Savage, guy?" Ed asked.

"The reports on this shaman are that he knows the secrets of the universe." This was a slight exaggeration, but I have found that stories were more interesting if you lingered on the edge of truth, rather then dive smack dab in the middle of it. This was not good reporting, but good story telling and at the moment I was telling a whopper of a story.

"Shaman," Ed repeated the word, probably not even knowing that it was the anthropological term for witchdoctor. You could tell just from his response to the sound of the word that he liked it.

"So, it's a deal?"

"Let me think about it," the editor fumed, but whenever he got to this point usually the deal was done. He probably needed to get prices from airports for airfares before he committed to anything.

"I'll check in later," I tacitly agreed to play the editor's game and turned. The wooden door with the large glass window was just starting to swing shut, as Perky had already bolted like a startled faun in the woods and was nowhere to be seen.

As I too left, closing the door behind me, I smiled with satisfaction. I, Norman Rock, had faced the dragon and at least held my own, but I knew I had to follow up before the day was over. I went to the restroom to splash some water on my face and gather my thoughts.

With cold water dripping down the sides of my checks, an Anglo-Saxon face looked back at me, my reddish brown hair framing hazel eyes, a well-proportioned nose, a good smile and a strong chin. This familiar visage stacked on top of a frame that just missed six feet was still youthful at the age of thirty, but looking as if I carried more wisdom than my age. Whether that was the case or not was another matter.

Although an anthropologist by profession, I had been without a job in my chosen field or any other profession, during the economic downturn in the early 1990s. I turned to the cutthroat world of journalism, proving myself by writing some local pieces on fires, politics and obituaries with a community-based newspaper in Massachusetts. Now here I was in 1993, trying to inch my way back to Anthropology, even though the path was slightly unconventional.

Who was the Noble Savage? I had heard obscure rumors about the Noble Savage from my anthropological contacts, who themselves only knew about him as rumors through others. He was more myth than man. Some of my peers wanted to go study his native philosophy, but the recent recession had cut the purse strings so much, the purse had to be thrown away. Ironically, the bad state of the economy left this opportunity open for me.

I can connect up with my old professor and arrange to do a monograph or something, while I am down there; I humored myself. Maybe this could lead to some doors being opened, and I could take up that doctoral program, which I could not afford previously. Hope was already building a new future for me.

I promised myself that in about two hours I would be back at Ed's door looking to finalize the arrangements. During the interim, I apprised Perky of Ed's proposed terms, obtaining an agreement that even though somewhat miserly, we would be able to abide by them. Right on time, I traipsed through the older newspaper building on course with destiny.

The vista of the newsroom opened before me. Across a large unbroken room were scattered thirty to forty desks, each in various states of disarray. Around this main room were smaller offices with walls that did not go up to the ceiling; these were given to the critical members of the newspaper, such as the owner, the editor, the assistant editor, the son of the owner, etc.

Purposely never modernized, these built-in cubicles were wooden, inset with large glass windows, so you could see in or out, depending upon your position in the room. Even the doors had a full pane of glass on their upper sections. Although some cigar smoke curled and intermingled in this picture, a hazy mist of paper specks swirled like a cloud across the room, giving the panorama a dusty-dreamy appearance.

Ed strategically positioned himself so he could peer out at his minions and onto every desk in the newsroom. Every one of the precious computer screens was turned so the editor could see it. All the other desks were still equipped with electric typewriters, though these were being phased out, reluctantly.

As I walked across the newsroom, Ed affixed me with his black eyes, while adjusting his heavy black rimmed glasses. He knew I was aiming towards his door. I completed the transit of the newsroom and just burst into his room. No use giving Ed an opportunity to say he was too busy to talk with me.

"Hi, Ed," I jauntily inquired, while knocking on the inside frame of the door as I entered. "What's the scoop?"

"Don't you know how to knock?" He grumbled.

"I did," I stated, emphasizing this with an additional knock of the desk, while I sat down in Ed's cushy leather chair that he kept for important personages. I was purposely being antagonistic. If Ed did not punish me with a tongue lashing for some reason, he might not feel I deserved to go and might stop me from going out of spite. So, I wanted to provide him with a good reason to give me a hard time, which he went on to do so, harping on politeness, etiquette and how to enter a room properly. I duly took the role of the chastened reporter. After he was finished his outburst, Ed settled into an uncomfortable stillness, which I let sit right there in the middle of the room like the stench of a rotten egg.

"Ok, in regards to this South America thing," Ed took a deep breath, after breaking the silence.

"So, you have an answer?"

"Yes, I expect you to come back with your shield or on it," the editor loved to throw in these allusions to ancient literature. In other words, he was ordering us like a Spartan general to get a few good stories on the Noble Savage's views—and some GOOD photographs—or die doing it. (Actually, on my first trip, I almost did just that!)

"That's great!" I would have jumped for joy, but knew if I did Ed would want to reduce my meal allowance again.

"And here are the tickets!" Ed handed over a packet. "You leave in a week!"

"Fantastic," I excitedly grabbed them, noticing references to boats. "These are tickets for an ocean liner?"

"Yeah," Ed smiled, which made me suspicious. "It will get you there in a couple of weeks, but I thought you would prefer to go on a cruise rather than fly."

"A cruise is good." I stated uncertainly, and then I realized, of course, Ed had succeeded in shafting us for two weeks without pay. This minor victory was the source of the smile, I imagined, and smiled back.

"They may ask you to perform some little duties, while on board," Ed's smile broadened.

"What duties?" I stiffened. There was obviously more to the story.

"Do you want the tickets or not? Ed put his hand out. "If not, give 'em back and we can put an end to this right now."

I had learned along the way in my study of Ed that he did not bluff, especially when he was talking about putting money back in his pocket. This was my one and only chance.

"I'll take them," I agreed, but I could not contain my anguish and frustration with Ed, expressed unequivocally through my body language. This discomfiture on my part titillated my editor to no end, proving in his mind that he had driven the harder bargain. Ed was in a good mood for the rest of the day.

We Discover the Noble Savage

The day finally arrived, when Perky and I showed up at the pier. There was a bright, shiny and BIG ocean liner next to a small beat-up freighter. My estimation of our editor, who had arranged for our tickets, soared! As we walked up the gangway of the bright, shiny vessel, our gait became jauntier and our heads bigger. A crisply attired officer on the boat's deck took our pack of tickets with a friendly nod.

"Sirs," the naval person nodded with a cordial smile, handing the packet of tickets back. "You are looking for the *SS Sea Galahad*."

"That's right!" Perky perked up before I could say anything. "And here we are."

"Well," the officer coughed, trying to disguise his laughter. With a jerk of his thumb, he gestured at the freighter further up the pier, which, I swear, was the dirtiest bucket of bolts on the ocean. "You want to go there."

As our step had risen (and our estimation of our editor with it) as we closed on the big, beautiful ocean liner, so did our emotions veer in the opposite direction with every dragging step as we ventured toward the *SS Sea Galahad*. You can only imagine what thoughts we harbored concerning the editor during the last steps towards this derelict vessel. (These thoughts were not fit for even salty ears.)

We were in awe that the contraption still floated, and I had some difficulty getting Perky up the gangway. I was as horrified as Perky at the vessel we were about to board, but I was also DETERMINED to get to South America, no matter what. Some seamen had to assist by picking Perky up and depositing him in a closet that they called a cabin. The Captain and

I assured the authorities that his prank was in terribly bad taste, when he yelled: "I am being kidnapped! Save me!"

Perky was seasick a great deal of the time, which he spent on the deck alternately vomiting and counting the sharks the whole way. Since I was the only able body, I had to perform not only my duties, but Perky's as well. These little chores were to help the cook with the cooking (I never want to see another potato), swab the decks and stoke the boiler. Working sixteen hour days, I estimate that the editor made money off my efforts. Certainly the captain did!

After a week aboard the *SS Sea Galahad*, we arrived at the head of the Orinoco River. Once on land, we scouted out the area. There were tales of fierce tribal actions upriver, including murder and cannibalism; being a hearty traveler, I loved the ambience of adventure, but Perky was of another mind. Ironically, he wanted to get back on the *SS Sea Galahad*. (Perky, this time had to be assisted *off* the boat by those nice seamen who now dumped him unceremoniously into the harbor.)

The next few days I was able to secure the service of two guides and two canoes, and off we embarked. Twenty days upriver we were surrounded by about ten dugout canoes filled with very agitated natives. The guide, who spoke the best English, said they were from the Yanomamo tribe. Even the guides were frightened, which did not contribute to my calm demeanor (the points of the tribesmen's spears stabbing my sides, drawing a profusion of blood, did not help my sense of security). My life appeared to be only moments away from ending. These yelling and screaming men, brandishing numerous weapons, became immediately subdued when they were told that we were there to find the Noble Savage. Their attitude changed from deadly to an unusual deference. They pointed further upriver and described a tributary to enter that they referred to as the 'disappearing river' in their language. The fearsome warriors depicted an almost mythical, but dangerous land. From that point on, these tribesmen never bothered us again. In fact these tribesmen avoided us as if we were voyaging to the land of the dead.

"What could cause such a change in behavior? Respect? Fear? Awe?" I wondered.

The reference to the disappearing river mystified us as we easily found the tributary that the Yanomamo had described. Our little crew rowed us up the little river for another day before we stopped at a roaring waterfall. There was now no other choice but to leave the canoes behind. Beaching the canoes, the four of us, the two guides, Perky and I, emptied the craft. Being near the end of the day, I had just started a camp, when Perky started yelling (he did a lot of that nowadays) that the canoes were gone. His concern was well founded as the guides had also disappeared, obviously taking the canoes with them. I was undaunted, since our need for the canoes had ended anyway. So, we camped and got started next day on foot.

"I thought palmetto only grew in the American Southwest," Perky pondered. With leaves slapping me in the face, I ignored his observations.

Here we were, beating our way through the thorny palmetto, as we approached our goal after five more days of bugs, snakes and jaguars. In my imagination the next thicket would bring us to the Noble Savage himself, but there were so many thickets that my imagination soon got exhausted. In my delusion or out of it, the chattering of human, not monkey, voices told us that a few steps more and we would be in the clearing where men made their homes. Hopefully, this would be the Noble Savage's village, but by this time our imagination did not care; any human habitation would do.

Bursting through a blind of thick, leafy vegetation, we found ourselves on a little knoll overlooking a bustling village nestled in a pristine one acre clearing. Over a dozen leaf-thatched circular buildings with white plaster walls were spread evenly over the area surrounded by the forest that looked like a massive green wall, speckled with a rainbow of brightly colored flowers and birds. The largest building of all was located in the center; this was the lone building that was rectangular and had an actual roof.

Like a Brueghel painting the village spread below us in a multi-level panoply of bustling people and animals, coming and going. The men were skimpily, but adequately clad in loincloths, but the women offended my civilized sensibility by wearing *just* loincloths, leaving their breasts visible for everyone to see. What a disgusting display! (I would complain when a woman came in to the office and breast fed her baby quietly in the corner. "She should do this in private." I declared at the time.)

One of these women was coming by us. Normally, my puritanical nature would dominate the focus of my attention, but for some reason all I could see were the eyes of this woman. I was bewitched. Not even her bouncing breasts could jostle my sensibilities away from her face.

"Excuse me," Perky hailed down the woman and then looked to me to take the lead. Unfortunately, I was leading nowhere as I was caught in the hypnotic gaze of this enchantress. Perky looked at me as if I had lost my mind. He had never seen me speechless before. Perky finally asked: "Do you know where the Noble Savage is?"

Shifting her gaze to Perky and releasing me from her spell, we could tell she did not understand Perky's words, but she seemed to know what we were looking for instantly. Pointing towards the center of the village, she nodded, indicating that we look there. Then she blocked our path and looked straight at me.

"Silesia," she pointed to herself.

"I believe she is giving us her name," Perky interpreted. Seeming not to be affected by this woman's magic, he pointed to himself and stated his own name,. "I'm Perky!"

When Silesia's gaze returned to me, I was dumb-struck–again. So Perky did the honors of saying "Norman" and pointed to me.

"Normaaan," Silesia repeated the name, smiled at me cryptically and then left. Perky broke the spell as he dragged my inert body toward the center of the village.

"What happened to you?" The puzzled youth queried.

"Nothing," I wanted to ignore the temporary insanity that had attacked me. I couldn't explain it, except that I was possibly in shock from the disgusting display of a hundred naked female breasts bouncing across the landscape.

Cropped short by a small herd of wild *shepker*, a sheep-like creature and a great lawnmower, the area about the round, domed *keevahs*, the indigenous population's standard dwelling, looked like a well-groomed rich man's lawn with naked children running, laughing, and playing some kind of game on it.

And there he was! Looking roughly 50 years old with a golden complexion, the Noble Savage was six-foot tall and thin. He looked upon our arrival with amusement. To the dismay of my puritanical Yankee background, he, too, was naked except for the traditional loincloth. (Can anthropologists have an opinion? Good thing I was a journalist and not an anthropologist on this jaunt. Forget the tenets of A *Free and Responsible Press!* Currently, a good journalist is expected to express strong opinions.) The Noble Savage's violet eyes were stunning.

Loafing under his favorite date palm, arms folded comfortably behind his head, bare left ankle over his equally bare–and hairy–right knee, the Noble Savage did not rise when he saw us come out of the brush, but indicated, with an amiable nod, some conveniently placed rocks. One got the impression he often entertained travelers searching for the meaning of life. Looking skeptically at the appointed rocks, I could have done with a comfortable, padded armchair myself, but, so what, I sighed internally, "when in Rome, do as the Romans do." That is, when in the jungle, do as the Noble Savages do.

"Hi, folks! Come sit a spell!" The Noble Savage stated to our surprise, inviting us in ENGLISH. "Take a load off your feet. What can I do for you fellers?" (I could swear that he spoke with an Irish accent.)

We wiped our sweaty brows and dropped our knapsacks in the dusty grass. With a brave smile, not to mention the shock of being addressed in English, I plopped down heavily on the rock. The bones in my bottom did not forgive the insult, and I winced. The Noble Savage nodded to a passing native, who quickly assessed our needs and brought two skins of *sasarpilla* juice made from the bright blue fruit waving over the edge of the river and two small juicy bright pink *melonas* from the encroaching jungle. The Noble Savage handed the leather skins filled with juice to me and my photographer. Propping his stand against the giant bole of a fragrant, flowering jungle tree and grabbing the leather pouch with a grateful grin, Perky swung the container up and drank heartily of the sapphire liquor.

The Noble Savage was an enigma, ageless, not young and not old. He appeared wise, but also somewhat child-like in his naïveté from my civilized perspective. Finally, he had a twinkle in his eye, which made one pause and think whether he was completely sincere or insincere.

The Noble Savage waited politely for my response as I gulped down the river-cooled *sasarpilla* and wiped my lips. Perky seemed to have swallowed his whole pouch in one gulp and was now greedily absorbing huge bites of *melona,* which a native girl had obligingly chopped up for him. (Where did she come from?)

"Thank you for the drink. I really needed that," I said to the Noble Savage. "You do not seem surprised by my arrival. Have you met a modern human like me, before?" I hated to think that another reporter had got here before me and stolen my story.

"Not in person, I haven't," the Noble Savage replied. "But I have long been aware of the existence of modern man."

"Then, how did you learn to speak English?"

Looking at the dense jungle surrounding us, no wires, no aerials in sight, I asked in amazement, "How?"

"By jungle telegraph, of course."

"Jungle telegraph? Drums?" I repeated dumbly, still seeing no cables or other communication devices anywhere about.

"Mostly bird-speak."

"Bird-speak?" I echoed.

"Of course. Very reliable. We have many bird-speakers fluent in bird talk of various suitable messenger species. We have bird-speakers posted about the edge of the jungle to pick up daily news from birds, which fly regularly to the cities of the Americas. Through bird-speak, we have learned thirty languages, including Spanish, Chinese, Russian, French, Portuguese and English."

"Never heard of such a thing," I scoffed at it.

"Bird-speak is more efficient than many of your supposedly more technical communications systems." The Noble Savage touted this unusual technology. "It's been used for thousands of years."

"That's got to be a joke," I exclaimed in disbelief.

"Why? Does it not fit your sense of modern communications? Bird-speak does not seem efficient or realistic in your opinion? I find you Moderns less illuminated than I expected. Bird-speak has done us so well that we have quite a library, including the *Bible* in seven languages. Now we complement bird-speak with a type of carrier pigeon, which brings in a newspaper regularly. And, we definitely know more about what is going on around the jungle than the urban dwellers on the coast."

"That is why the woman we asked for help knew to send us to you?" I hesitantly pondered.

"Yes, the tribe has been waiting for you to arrive." The Noble Savage smiled. "We prepared a *keevah*, one of the tribal huts, for each of you several days ago, but since you insisted on going in circles in the brush, the *keevahs* have been gathering dust, waiting for you.

"Then you already know why I'm here, and what I want to find out," I challenged him. Perky had quietly slipped away, while we were talking. This young man knows the better part of valor and that is the part that gets him to a place where he can socialize with young women.

"Not in complete detail, but, yes, you are a reporter and his photographer; you are here to do a set of articles on me." The Noble Savage confirmed. "Since it serves our own purposes to give you that information, the tribe agreed to let you in on our secret existence. If they hadn't, we would never have met. I and my tribe would have melted like ghosts into the shadows and the mists, and the river would have disappeared from the face of the Earth."

"Why does it serve your purpose?" I ignored his extreme and obviously primitive assertions. Must be some belief in magic that I have not delved into as of yet.

"As a warning to you Moderns that you have encroached upon our ancient territory and to encourage you to come no closer," the Noble Savage said.

"Oh, yes, and if we don't heed your warning," I taunted insolently. "What then?"

"Look up," he said, and pointed to a cloud-obscured mountain peak. "The god of that mountain will cover you with lava and burn every tree to cinders before you can take a cutting machine to it. It will be centuries before this area is useful again, but we will be safely away."

"Don't tell me the mountain takes orders from you as to when it will erupt!"

"I won't," the Noble Savage promised, "But I assure you it will erupt, when I say it will do so. Behold!"

The Noble Savage pointed sharply to the mountain. As if to underline what he had said, a long spume of fire and smoke spurted from the volcano's crest. Clouds formed from the hot steam. No use arguing about whether or not magic existed; I put the matter aside and got down to business.

"We come as ambassadors of good will," I stated loftily, "We seek knowledge of your laws, customs and philosophy, for unless we know them, we might inadvertently tread on your toes—uh, break your rules, and offend your traditions."

"Nothing wrong with gaining wisdom," the Noble Savage said cheerfully, "but I think you are too weary to go into such details today. Tomorrow is soon enough. Let me escort you to your *keevahs*." He gestured towards a *keevah* where a cluster of young women were laughing and giggling. Perky was at the center of this gaggle of females, taking pictures, laughing and teasing. They seemed fascinated by his unruly ringlets of fiery red hair.

"Good heavens!"

"I'm workin', boss," Perky raised up his camera. "I'm workin'!"

When one girl stood on tiptoe to touch his carrot top, he grabbed the maiden and kissed her (Did she allow him to kiss her? Or, heavens, did she force the kiss on Perky? I could not tell. Of course, Perky did not attempt to resist the effort whatsoever.). I must have a talk with that young man about sex as soon as we are alone in the *keevah*. I yawned. That is, I would lay the law down about strictly non-sexual behavior for junior photographers on special assignments, if I didn't fall asleep first.

On the Noble Savage

The next day proved to be beautiful. We enjoyed ideal weather while surrounded by the vibrant green forest. The flawlessly tended village appeared to exist within a green bubble as the towering trees arched overhead, blotting out any view of the sky. Pink *melonas*, purple orchids and yellow fruit dotted this green-hazed, leaf-encrusted vision. Bright blue, red and yellow birds flitted from tree to tree. In the middle of this immaculate village lay the Noble Savage, resting within a hammock, swaying to the passing wind, as if he were the center of the universe.

"How are you this morning?" I started the conversation off without too much ado.

"I am fine," The Noble Savage stated rather pleasantly. "Do you feel rested now?"

"Much–," I hesitated, not knowing if I should enter into my questions right away or pass some more pleasantries back and forth.

"You must have a thousand questions," The Noble Savage read the situation perfectly. "Why don't we start with your first question and see where it leads?"

"Well, I was wondering why you call yourself the Noble Savage," I took his cue and took off.

"Actually, I don't," the Noble Savage corrected me. "Through bird-speak, the tribe heard about the concept of the Noble Savage and, although he never used the term itself, Rousseau's development of the concept interested them. For some reason, someone connected me to this idea and started calling me that. I objected, but no one listened. Eventually, the practice spread outside the tribe, and now it is impossible to stop."

"Sorry, I'm late!" Suddenly, Perky appeared with a couple of young ladies in tow. Snapping off a couple of pictures, he sat down on the all too familiar rock in the clearing. He looked unsure, thinking that maybe he should be part of the conversation, but reluctantly so. "What're you talking about?"

"I was clarifying that my name is not really the Noble Savage."

"All this way and you are not the right guy?" Perky asked, horrified that he might have to pick up his gear and go back into the bushes.

"No," the Noble Savage responded. "Many call me the Noble Savage, but I don't call myself that."

"Why do you think the people around here started referring to you as the Noble Savage?" I asked.

"I have no idea, but I have speculated on it." The Noble Savage replied. "Rousseau said the Noble Savage was pretty much a proto-human, who would be, and I quote, 'wandering through the forest without industry, without words, without a home, without wars and without needing the companionship of his fellow creatures, nor the desire to bother them.' That passage is from his *Discourse on the Origin of Inequality*."[1]

"I don't think you qualify," I agreed looking around at the village, although quite impressed at his act of memory.

"Yah, and where do you fit women in that picture?" Perky asked, scratching his head. "Women like – companionship!"

"Yes, I would not think I qualify as homeless." The Noble Savage waved at the *keevahs*. "But, really, no human qualifies. The Noble Savage concept has sometimes been associated with tribes in the South Pacific, Africa and the American West, but all these tribes had social structures far more complex than what Rousseau was talking about."

"Doesn't make much sense," I shook my head.

"Rousseau said a lot about the Noble Savage, but he was wrong." The Noble Savage stated. "Most humans must belong to some sort of social order: a place to call home, a way to communicate and, of course, some system to gather food and propagate."

"I would call that list the most basic of basics," I allowed.

"Among others, Rousseau had two main elements that he attributed to the Noble Savage, the ability to integrate the Noble Savage's desires transparently within the context of his universe and a sense of freedom, which the civilized man does not have."

"This is a little heavy for my normal reading public," I admitted, though I rushed to take it all down.

"I call it boring." Perky was already losing his focus.

---

1   Rousseau, *Discourse on the Origin of Inequality*, p. 66, translated from the French by Carmen S. Barraford.

I gave Perky a glance that wilted the purple flowers around him, but he was oblivious. Perky only had eyes for the young women who had busied themselves by getting drinks and waving palm fronds to keep Perky in comfort.

"Then let us take this discussion a point at a time." The Noble Savage got up from his hammock and stretched. "Rousseau's first point is well-founded. Basically, a savage knows he is a savage and is happy with what he has. There is no such thing as social status to twist his mind."

"I don't see anything wrong with social status," I was a little confused. "I like knowing if I am a better reporter than John, and I know that with bigger headlines and bylines."

"See, we differ here, I suppose," the Noble Savage picked up a leather of *sasarpilla* and drank, while I waited anxiously for him to finish his thought. "As far as I am concerned, this place is paradise. Paradise is not an illusory position in a social structure. My sense of happiness integrates my environment, my consciousness and my body into a whole. My happiness is now, because there is nothing more I need to fulfill my happiness. Are you happy now?"

"I have to finish these articles," I prevaricated. "Then, they have to be published on the first page of the newspaper and then, if I am lucky, the calls will start coming in extolling their virtues, making my series of articles a fabulous success. When that happens, I will be happy."

"A lot of 'ifs' and 'thens' before you find happiness," the Noble Savage noted. "Your sense of happiness is in the future, contingent on a lot of things happening in a particular way, and, of course, as you get closer to your happiness more future 'ifs', 'ands' and 'buts' will pop up pushing your happiness even further into the future. You may actually glimpse happiness and have an occasional euphoric moment believing that you have finally attained happiness, but in reality you never did."

"I remember being happy," I responded defensively.

"Possibly when you were a child," the Noble Savage suggested. "Sometimes, children experience happiness like noble savages before society comes along and tells them it is wrong. Of course, most young children don't have to worry about where their next meal comes from and the urge to procreate has not started."

"I must have attained happiness," I reached for straws. "I once fell in love and it was wonderful. I think I was happy then."

"Are you still in love?" The Noble Savage inquired. "Are you still with the lady?"

"No, we drifted apart and ended up never marrying." I admitted, adding almost wistfully. "I haven't seen the woman in years."

"So, you luxuriated in a blissful emotion and when it got used up; then you were no longer in love, from what I gather." The Noble Savage inquired.

"In a way," I admitted reluctantly.

"You think happiness is an act of consumption, while I feel it is a state of mind." The Noble Savage speculated, but with an uncanny accuracy.

"At any moment, I can crystallize my thoughts and my life and realize I am happy and believe it at my most profound levels of thought. Can you? Can you say that you are happy now?"

"Happy? Now?" I replied, astonished. "How can I be?"

"My sense of happiness is continuous, cumulative and can be tapped at any time." The Noble Savage continued. "Your concept of happiness is broken in bits and pieces spread across a somewhat shattered personal cosmos. My conclusion is that a modern civilized man can never be truly happy."

"I'm happy," I said defensively. "Once I get these articles done, I could be famous and rich."

"Fame and fortune have no bearing on happiness; they are just the largest *melona* hanging in the highest tree." The Noble Savage smiled. "Your happiness is the pursuit of happiness, which can be a never-ending vicious cycle. I am glad to be a savage."

"I'm happy," I insisted limply, but in the back of my mind these thoughts flashed like a lighthouse beam sweeping over a bay, as I started to doubt my own thoughts. I thought to myself; remember, this fellow is a savage. *I* am the civilized one here.

For some reason, now that I was away from modern society, I tended to discount my disillusionment, my profound dissatisfaction, and extol the virtues of my distant memory. Modern society was transformed into this perfect order against which I was to measure the rest of reality.

"I got to go!" Perky blurted out and jumped up, waving his camera and wildly snapping off some pictures.

"What are you doing?" I uttered my displeasure in the tonalities of my voice. Inwardly I was relieved that Perky's disconnected contributions to our conversation would depart with him. This Noble Savage was being too nosy, as far as I was concerned, and I did not want any distractions as I talked with him.

"Got to get the lay of the land," Perky responded. I was not too pleased with the subtle implications in his response. After he took about ten scattered shots, not even looking at where the camera was directed, he took off again, as abruptly as he had arrived.

"Let's move on to Rousseau's second item about freedom." The Noble Savage continued, watching the young man disappear into the forest. "He said that the detritus of society, the accumulation of society's rules, written and unwritten, are invisible chains that imprison every civilized person."

"Yes," I was happy the Noble Savage had changed the direction of the conversation, compensating for my unhappiness that Perky was not being responsible. (Were Perky's work habits one of the conditions to my happiness? I didn't want to think about it.) "I am from the land of the free, and as far as I am concerned, that is garbage."

"I agree with you." The Noble Savage *agreed* with me! I was shocked that we had some thoughts in common.

"The foundations of freedom and happiness are the basic rules, which a society formulates, to prevent strife from happening." The Noble Savage continued. "Rousseau implies this set of rules in the quote that I gave you earlier. For instance, the Noble Savage was a 'stranger to war' and had no desire to hurt his fellow savages. This implies that the Noble Savage abided by the rule that 'thou shalt not kill'. Underneath Rousseau's definition lingers a primitive version of the *Bible's* Ten Commandments."

"So, Rousseau's Noble Savage did have some basic rules he had to abide by; he had some chains just like civilized man."

"Yes, in theory, but I believe Rousseau's imprecise focus was on the number of chains." My host pressed a finger to his mouth thoughtfully, and then pointed the finger at me. "You are a civilized man, correct? What is your ethical foundation?"

"Well," I guessed, taken somewhat aback. "Being from a Judeo-Christian background, I would start with the Ten Commandments and add an eleventh commandment from Jesus Christ's teachings to do by others as you would have them do by you. Then, I would add the American Bill of Rights."

"Your foundation is getting pretty complicated," the Noble Savage noted. "And with every new level of complexity, the possible number of interpretations increases exponentially."

"I suppose," I started to wonder who was running this interview.

"Beyond your documented foundation do you have other unwritten social rules?"

"Such as?"

"If you own a home, how about mowing the lawn?"

"There is no law about mowing lawns, everyone is free to grow their grass as long as they like, but the neighbors might not be happy about that."

"So there is an unwritten rule to mow the lawn," the Noble Savage pressed on. "Or you make your neighbors unhappy."

"Yes—No," I was uncertain.

"This is just a mundane, probably poor, example, but you see the difference in magnitude between the savage working with a foundation of just five or so commandments in comparison to the civilized man's complex web work?"

"So the savage is a man with a very simple set of rules for life and social interactions." I summed up our conversation.

"Correct," the Noble Savage stated, unequivocally.

"Where does the noble fit?"

"A person who truly lives and believes in his or her basic rules without being a hypocrite is noble. A kindred soul to Rousseau, Diogenes of Sinope went abroad with a lamp and when asked what he was doing he said he was in search of an honest man, basically a man without hypocrisy. He never found one."

"So, what is not noble is a man with numerous ethical rules, to which he can adhere to only a portion due to convenience or in some cases just a discontinuity in his or her logic?"

"Civilization is a patina that tarnishes the nobility of man." The Noble Savage confirmed. "Civilized man is so far from nobility that he does not know what noble is anymore, which is why the concept is so fascinating to modern man. Living up to ten laws is easy compared to living up to thousands of conflicting rules, most of which are unwritten."

"Being noble is much easier for a savage then it is for a civilized man." I had to admit.

"Rousseau was romanticizing the concept of a Noble Savage like most civilized people," The Noble Savage smiled. Somehow I thought he was tweaking my nose. "Using this criterion, I am truly happy and I live comfortably with my primitive number of commandments, but the cornerstone of my commandments is to respect all other living creatures. So, I guess I am the real thing, a Noble Savage and I presume the people around here thought the same. Why else would they have started calling me that?"

Our Little Talk

Morning is a magical time. The Noble Savage, for that was all I knew to call him at the moment, even if it were not his name, had arranged for both Perky and me to hike into the foothills of what I suspected were the Guiana Highlands to see a waterfall and wait for the sun to arise.

We traipsed through the leftovers of the night with the Noble Savage leading the way. The journey was a nightmare of jungle vines and grass, clinging to us, as if the vegetation was trying to pull us back into the gloom. After what seemed like hours, the birds began their morning chirps, and we could hear what sounded like thunder in the pale darkness. Then the trail began to go up a steep rise, while the vegetation started to become sparser. We were all fatigued, even the indefatigable Noble Savage was showing signs of exertion, but shortly we came to a misty clearing, which the Noble Savage indicated to us was our destination. With each step a rumbling sound increased.

Whether due to the exertion or thundering noise, no one in our party spoke. We all just listened to the rumble and the occasional loud bird, screaming higher up the mountain as they saw the light we could not see of the advancing dawn. The thunder felt as if it was all around us, under our feet, above our heads and on all sides.

Looking about, I realized that I was at an elevated level, a few hundred feet above the canopy of the rain forest just below me. Although gloomy, this gray-slate sky was a novelty, since the rain forest rarely gave broad glimpses of this usually glorious blue mantel.

As the light arrived, the brilliant blue of the sky overlaid a scene of blue water and green verbiage. The clearing before me contained a pool about thirty feet across and this was fed by a small, thin waterfall that came down from above. This was the source for the pool and the constant mist. Above and below, the water pounded down.

Beyond, I beheld a spectacular panorama that kept me enthralled. Across a cavernous ravine, there was a broad waterfall about a quarter mile across with several steps dropping four hundred feet, glistening in the pink of the dawn, rainbows shimmering like fantastic jewelry across the waterfall's brow. In silence I watched and listened. I don't know how long I was spellbound, but an eternity of water, thoughts and life passed before me.

"I'm hungry?" The Noble Savage finally broke the spell by shouting these words over the noise of the waterfall.

"Me, too!" Perky responded immediately, as if the Noble Savage's words broke our noisy, but contemplative cosmic bubble.

"Go down the path away from this waterfall," The Noble Savage yelled, indicating the thin waterfall plunging down from above and pointed down a path bending around the cliff. "It is time to get out of this mist."

This is when I realized that I was soaked from the constant mist in the clearing. Dew drops rippled across my skin and the fabric of my clothes were drenched.

"Perky, Norman," the Noble Savage pressed on. "The next clearing down that path is much drier; Collect some wood and start a fire, while I get our breakfast."

The Noble Savage nodded at the pool and I understood that he was going to do a little fishing. Although I wanted to see him fish, I was not in the mood to argue, as the chill of the mist was sinking in with a vengeance. Off we went and in twenty minutes we had a fire going in another, smaller clearing. Between the warmth of the day and the heat of the fire, I was soon dried off. I could still see about half of the main waterfall. Not fifteen minutes later, the Noble Savage showed up, clutching a half dozen fish held together with a string made from woven vines. Soon he had the fish cleaned, spitted and hanging over the fire as he warmed his hands.

"The big waterfall is a glorious sight," the Noble Savage said. "But we have to go twenty-three miles to see it."

"Why don't you move here?" Perky inquired, still enamored with the spectacle. "What a great view!"

"Fishing and hunting on a cliff-side is not as fruitful as the plenty provided by the rain forest." The Nobel Savage still had to speak loudly, even though the main part of the waterfall's thunder was left back in the misty clearing. "The tribe can maintain a balance between what we use and the resources of the rain forest, but we cannot do that here. The continuity of life is predicated on not disrupting the balance."

"Balance, yes," I caught at the opportunity to bring up an issue, which had been stewing between Perky and me. "Talking about balance, we need to maintain a balanced relationship with the Noble Savage and his people."

"Balanced?" Perky cocked his head, not knowing what I was talking about. Carrying a bright red head of hair, Perky was in general an excellent photographer and a good lad. Like many people, he has a strength, which is also his weakness. He is very inquisitive, but this can lead down some unusual and profitable paths or create various distractions, since he has an extremely short attention span.

"We must maintain a balanced perspective," I puffed myself up in my own importance. "I expect you to adjust your behavior accordingly."

"I still don't know what you are talking about," Perky pushed back his red hair.

"I think he wants you to stay away from the girls," The Noble Savage joined in, amused by my stodginess.

"That's it," I agreed. "Don't view the people in the clearing as men and women; they are our subjects."

"We are like fish in a bowl," the Noble Savage interjected, but not with as much ardor as I would like. Was there a touch of sarcasm in the Noble Savage's statement?

"Exactly," I agreed. "They are not to be touched, only observed."

"You are like the omniscient eye of God," the Noble Savage continued with a little more levity than I expected.

"I wouldn't go as far as that," I corrected, "but we need to maintain a distance from our subjects."

"Aren't you setting yourself up for a very lonely visit with us?" The Noble Savage asked with some compassion.

"I need to work with them," Perky spoke up with a verve that he rarely had shown. "They are showing me places that I cannot find without them, and they are helping me get some great photos."

"I am sure they are showing you some interesting sites," I agreed readily. "Some of those sights may be too interesting."

"They are grown women," the Noble Savage argued. "And Perky, at least in physique, is a grown man."

"That's what I am worried about!" I admitted. "To intermingle the civilized with the savage is just not done! This is the civilized way to proceed!"

In the end, I pretended that I made my point. The Noble Savage looked upon me sadly, and Perky went on as if this conversation had never happened.

On Homo Sap

A new day had dawned and the early morning sunlight filtered through the leaves, glistening on a rising mist to create a green hazy world. Walking through this green haze was like sauntering through a dream.

"Now, Noble Savage," I started in today quickly, pressing to find some reality in this idyllic miasma. "If your real name is not the Noble Savage, what is it?"

"In our world, my real name is sacred and carries much spiritual power, so I cannot give it to you. I apologize." He got up into a sitting position in his hammock.

"Since you don't even call yourself the Noble Savage, what should I call you?" I pondered.

"I am a great admirer of Homer's *Odyssey* and in that tome Ulysses gives his name to the Cyclops, who imprisoned him in a cave, as Nemo, which means Nobody. How about calling me Nobody?"

"I can't write an article where that person's name is Nobody." I looked at him a little cock-eyed. "People would think I am writing an Abbot and Costello script. Nobody is on first, now Nobody is on second base…"

"Let's see," the Noble Savage put his elbow on his knee and rested his chin against his fist. He looked for a moment like Rodin's statue *The Thinker*. "I don't want to embarrass you. Alternatively, I was thinking you could call me Man, since most societies refer to themselves in their own language as such, but I don't think your readers would think that to be imaginative, and I am sure you want our readers to think I am clever."

"We must be clever," I agreed. "But not too clever. My editor tells me we are writing to 4th grade readers. Keep the multi-syllabic words to a minimum." (Oops, the multi-syllabic words just keep slipping out!)

"How about this? Man is known as Homo sapiens, but I feel that is presumptuous, so why don't you call me Homo Sap. My children always said I must be of another species."

"Don't you know the cross-lingual pun involved there?" I asked cautiously. Homo Sap was better than Nobody, so I was not ready to argue with him too much.

"I know the implications very well." He acknowledged. "As you know, Homo sapiens, relating to the modern human species, means intelligent, wise or sapient human (an oxymoron, if I ever heard one). When my Dad made an error, he used to rap his head and groan: 'How could I have been so daft? Tis not a Homo sapiens I am, just a stupid sap!' meaning he was a fool."

"People might think of Homo Sap as some strange local name." In comparison to the first choice, Nobody, Homo Sap looked really good. Desperately, I rationalized the use of this odd name to myself. "Was it possible that the Noble Savage could see through my arrogance about being civilized and my occasional sarcasm that I considered some of his answers less than sapient, and rather uncivilized?"

"In fact, my Dad considered our whole tribe Homo saps," the Noble Savage pronounced proudly. "We are all saps, but I am the biggest sap of them all!"

"I wouldn't say that," I wavered out of politeness.

"You can call me Sap for short," the Noble Savage announced, amused at the cringing response he had elicited from me.

"I don't know about that," I hesitated, but the Noble Savage, Homo Sap, had made up his mind and one thing I have found out about Homo Sap is that once his mind is made up, there is no changing it. A decision is a decision: irrevocable and without regrets. A civilized man knows you have to regret every decision you make, even if it was the right one.

In the end, I fell prey to calling him the Noble Savage, since he was a far better representative of the concept then Rousseau ever imagined, but I used Homo Sap, also, to keep him happy.

On Justice

"How can we save our children from moral destruction by our own institutions?" I gabbled, while Perky and Homo Sap were feasting on newly caught fish and freshly harvested fruit near the main building. "How can we bring them back to a state of Noble Savagery like yours?"

Homo Sap grinned. "Those terms are dichotomous. You can be a savage, but not be noble or you can be a savage **and** be noble."

"Well Rousseau said...," I protested.

"Did Rousseau ever live among real, genuine savages?" Homo Sap asked.

"No," I had to admit. Rousseau was an intellectual during the French Enlightenment, dying in 1788. "He only left Europe once to visit England, but I am sure that this qualified for the French at the time as living among Ignoble Savages."

"A savage may be noble in bearing, in manners, or in heart, depending on what you mean by noble." Homo Sap ignored my sorry joke. "Or he may be a clumsy oaf, who gets his kicks from beating his dog, his child, his wife or anybody else he can lay hands on."

"Really!" Perky and I protested in unison. "You make it sound as if a savage is no different from a civilized man."

"He isn't. If he's a member of a family or a tribe, he's got a civilization which governs how he mates, treats his brothers, his children or his pack."

"Now you make civilized man sound no better than an animal."

"He isn't; he's worse. The cruelty of a savage stems from instinct or fear. Any animal will bite, if it fears you. Man's cruelties are premeditated. Many men and women enjoy perpetrating acts of mental and physical torture upon others. Why, I've seen some of our neighbors laugh all day about how a sacrificial victim screamed for mercy as the shaman flayed off his skin, or how a law-breaker squirmed in agony on the stake until it pierced his heart."

"We are too civilized to make human sacrifices," I retorted, hotly defending modern civilization.

Homo Sap looked surprised. "You don't? I have heard you still offer living sacrifices to your god, Justice."

"Yes, in a way," I admitted, thinking about the criminal that was executed quite recently in one of our more benighted states. The United States, I thought proudly, is more civilized than *that*, "but only convicted criminals."

"And the god Justice never makes mistakes?"

"Ugh—well—not often—"

"And if a mistake is made, does the god Justice resurrect his victim and repay him for his pains, his despair?"

"No—how could he—I mean Justice is an abstract—that is, it doesn't really exist—well, it can't—"

"Then why do you have a system for Justice? Why do you make sacrifices to Justice?"

"I keep telling you we do not make sacrifices to Justice—"

"Oh, you just kill legally in the name of your god, Justice?"

"Don't keep saying that! We do **not** kill in the name of Justice. We execute criminals who have been legally condemned to death."

"But if Justice has no real existence, what else is an execution except a murder which has been condoned by the people and vicariously committed by all the people?"

"Don't confuse us. Justice **does** exist. It's the name of a product of a code of acceptable human behavior with penalties for disobedience, which civilized humans have imposed on themselves."

"Subject to change according to the level of civilization you have reached, I suppose," Homo Sap observed thoughtfully.

"That's it!" I commented, grateful for his understanding.

"Ah! So your civilization has progressed to a stage beyond sacrificial killings to the god or gods, with the exception of your god Justice."

I stepped right into the trap.

"That's right. Except our executions are not killings."

"No," Perky blurted out; (I do wish that boy wouldn't poke his nose in, where it isn't wanted! His job is to take pictures and keep his mouth shut.) "They are a legal punishment of felons."

"The felons still die, don't they?"

"Yes."

"Then their deaths are killings."

On the defensive, we both squirmed as if staked out on an anthill. "But our executions are not unusual or anything–It's all very scientific and cool–we don't hang, shoot, decapitate, administer lethal drugs or electrocute anyone in an inhumane way. Someone always oversees the execution to see it is correctly performed. We don't hurt the criminal excessively—"

"If you died whether you were purposely strangled, shot, had your head chopped off, were forcibly poisoned, or fried by a bolt of lightning, it wouldn't hurt you excessively?"

"You're twisting everything we say around," I accused.

"I'm just pointing out that Justice is one of the institutions which your civilization has created, an environment where any sadists among you are able to insinuate themselves into positions where they can contemplate and commit with relish, cold-blooded, premeditated murder without shuddering or shame."

"Okay, smarty pants!" I shouted, "How would your tribe handle a vicious criminal?"

"Remember, I am just a Noble Savage?" he taunted, "Pure in heart and all that? So, if I and my tribal members are so pure and don't have morally destructive institutions to spoil us, why would our society have any criminals?"

"You don't have any criminals?" Perky and I were taken aback.

"Of course we do. We're human. Make a law, and we'll break it, just like you, but we put a high price on our lives and liberty. We must live free or die."

"Oh, ho," we chorused in satisfaction. I relentlessly pursued this point. "If someone takes a life in your society, you make them pay, too."

"We sure do," Homo Sap admitted. "If one man kills another, he has to support that man's wife, children, brothers, sisters, parents, grandparents, or in-laws, whoever was dependent on that victim, emotionally or financially, for the rest of his life."

"That's slavery!" we gasped. "That's inhuman."

"So was the deed. Many criminals beg on their knees to get off with a one-time monetary payment, or even for death. But that's up to the victim's relatives. If they say no, a slave that killer is, until they change their minds. Of course, if the killer insists on death, that has to be approved by the victim's family. One of the family members must do the dirty deed in front of all of us. Why should the rest of society, or the state, have blood-sullied hands?"

I was baffled.

"Do many victims' relatives take matters into their own hands and execute a murderer?"

"Not many. Most say killing is too good for such murderous felons. Let them live and suffer for their crimes. Death gives them a peace they don't deserve. It teaches them nothing. Life does."

Perky and I were both silent, mulling over this odd kind of justice. Homo Sap smiled at us kindly.

"Noble Savages aren't completely savage," he assured us. "If the felon is young, we make his teachers pay part of the price in his place, for not bringing their student up to respect the life and property of others."

"Since you are a Noble Savage," I pointed out disgustedly, "what is the basic tenet of your primitive society?"

"*Noblesse oblige*," Homo Sap replied promptly. "Since we all must rely on each other, it's the only way we can survive. It's something like the buddy system you fellers use when you go swimming. One helps the other. Those who were born, through no effort of their own, with greater strength, skill or intelligence, know it's their duty to use their gifts for the benefit of those born with less."

"Oh, God," I groaned, "another do-gooder!"

"Not exactly," Homo Sap declared. "It's our overweening pride."

"How do you mean pride?"

Homo Sap pointed to a tall, stoic warrior on duty nearby. A vicious little brat was kicking the man's brawny bare legs with his alligator leather sandals. The man made no sign that he either saw the little creep beside him, felt the child's sturdy sandal blows or heard his shrill insults.

"Is it a ritual trial of strength or endurance?" I asked, puzzled by the warrior's immobility. Perky was looking at the warrior's broad pectorals with youthful masculine envy. (Not that I blamed him. The pair of us should work out at the gymnasium more often. In comparison, we were both a bit out of shape. Is being out of shape part of being civilized?) "Why doesn't he give the child a dose of his own medicine and kick back?"

"It *is* a kind of test," Homo Sap admitted. "Ask him about it."

So we strolled over to the warrior.

"Why do you let that kid kick you?" I asked.

The proud warrior looked down at us disdainfully and spoke, "He is a child. I am big, powerful, and a fearless warrior. He cannot hurt me. Why should I punish him for being a child who knows no better?"

My comrade pushed back his cap and scratched his head. I stroked my chin thoughtfully and remarked pensively, "We don't get it."

Homo Sap smiled. "That's all right, boys. Don't worry about it. You will get it, if you and your tribe let yourselves live long enough to grow up."

Version of the Expulsion From Eden

Homo Sap warned us. "Views differ as to what really happened when Adam and Eve were expelled from Eden. It's only natural. When several people recount an event, there are bound to be discrepancies."

"Like journalism, where you need to have two or more sources reaffirm the same story to have confidence that the story is true," I volunteered.

"Yes, very astute, I can tell you are civilized." I could not tell if Homo Sap was being sarcastic or not; I assumed that, as a savage, he was not advanced enough to know what sarcasm was. "One thing is clear, however," he went on. "God is good and would never abuse His children. God doted on His very first human child, but like other fond parents, found out that too much, too soon, could–and did–turn Adam into a spoiled brat."

"For example, when Adam whined that he was lonesome, God made him a wife from another batch of *humus*—soil, you know. That's why people are called humans," Homo Sap explained. "*Human* doesn't mean 'Huh, You Man or Male'. It just means 'thing made out of dirt, or humus.' That's why we say, 'Ashes to ashes; Dust to dust!' at a funeral—because, devoid of its life force, that's all a corpse is, ashes or dust."

"The first Eve—'eve' isn't a name, it just means woman, a version of *ewe*, or female—was not to Adam's taste (as I recall vaguely, her name was Lamia or the like). He couldn't get it up with her, he said. She wasn't pretty or sexy enough. So that spoiled brat, Adam, wailed some more and stamped his feet, and God said, Alright! Alright! No more noise. I'll make some one prettier or sexier for you, as soon as I finish creating these galaxies."

"Then God made Adam a second wife. (*I don't know what he did with the first one, Homo Sap never told me.*) This one was a vivacious, sexy temptress called Lilith. And still Adam wasn't satisfied. Lilith was a liberated woman, who wouldn't let him have his own way all the time. She wanted a career in magic. She wanted equal rights with Adam. She wouldn't cook or clean, if he wouldn't do his share —and he wouldn't. He wanted Lilith to do it all."

"I'm not a doormat," she screamed at him, "and I absolutely refuse to have children, because they take up too much time, and I'm too busy having fun, making magic and casting spells."

"So Adam went to God again, whining and grousing about that witch, Lilith. (If I had been God, I would have given Adam a time-out for bad behavior and told him to put up with Lilith. But then, I'm only a mean, nasty human. Heck, I might even have slapped the kid's behind!)"

"God, being all compassionate, as well as All Loving, coddled His son's tantrums and created Mother Eve from Adam's fifth rib–although He did say firmly that this was the *very last time* He would make Adam another playmate."

"Mother Eve, Adam's third wife, lived happily with Adam for uncounted time in the eternal Garden of Eden, until Lucifer or Satan entered Eden in the guise of a Serpent, tempting Adam's woman to eat the fruit of the Tree of Knowledge. This fruit had been expressly forbidden to Adam and Eve, because, *God knew*, knowledge without a sense of honor and responsibility is like a potent medicine. Used wisely, it can heal; used for the wrong reasons, it can kill. God knew Adam and Eve were not ready for that responsibility."

"Take nuclear power: the first thing your people did with this awesome force was to make an atomic bomb and kill a lot of innocent people with it. Except for a few Noble Savages, hidden in a remote jungle, who live according to Natural Law, your civilization has tainted the world." Homo Sap pointed out with a significant lift of one eyebrow. "People in your contaminated world do not use weapons to protect themselves from wild beasts or to kill game for food; you use this knowledge to kill each other. You learn how to grow food or make money, and then won't share either the food or the money."

"No need to make such a big deal about it, Sap—er–Homo Sap," I said crossly, "You make everyone outside your blessed Garden—that is jungle, look as greedy as a horde of thieving packrats."

"Not all," Homo Sap corrected me. "But enough of you to show that no matter how much you learn, it won't do you any real good until you learn how to use knowledge for the benefit of everyone."

I longed to call him a smart ass, but I'm too civilized, plus it is not wise to alienate the source of one's articles. My editor has rules about quarreling with the people I interview, so I merely asked, almost calmly: "Then why do you savages think yourselves so much better than us?" (I left out the noble on purpose. I was still mad at him.)

"A matter of choice," Homo Sap averred. "We aren't better than you. Occasionally, we just made a few wiser choices. Remember, although God gave His children Free Will, He denied them access to that Golden Apple, because He knew they were too young to handle that much knowledge. He wanted to keep them in the Garden until they were mature enough to make the right decisions. Some versions of this story claim He threw them out in a fit of uncontrolled anger. But God is perfect. Man is not. God *never* gets out of temper, like an imperfect human." Homo Sap shook his head at such an irreverent depiction of the All Perfect, Almighty One.

"What really happened," he said, "was that the guilty pair ***was afraid that* God *would throw them out*** for their sins. Hearing voices and glimpsing an Angel with a Flaming Sword, they panicked and ran, not waiting to figure out what the Angel was saying. They fled from Eden, Adam yelling back over his shoulder like a peevish baby, Its Eve's fault! The woman made me do it! She made me eat the apple!"

"Eve got back at Adam by snidely remarking that God was particularly grieved that Man, made in God's image, was a buck passer."

(Homo Sap didn't say how she knew this!—about God being grieved that Adam was blaming someone else for his own shortcomings, that is.)

"True," Homo Sap went on, "Eve had behaved badly, too. But wasn't she made of the same clay as Adam? Flesh of the same flesh, she shared his vices and his virtues, what few he has. By this act of cowardice in not facing up to the consequences of their actions, they left their immortality in the Garden and moved into the earthly realm of time and change, growth and decay."

"God sighed when He heard Adam yelling and said; No matter how many millions of years it takes, the children of Adam and his inquisitive mate, Eve, must grow up on one of my enigmas, Earth, and show Me they are fit for Heaven before I let them back in."

"You might say," Homo Sap concluded whimsically, "that Adam and Eve, this foolish pair of spoiled children, had it all and threw it away. I hope that even if we adults aren't as innocent of evil as the wild animals are that our children will be smarter."

(I almost squirmed under Homo Sap's look. Did the man have second sight? Did he know about that instance in my childhood when I hadn't been smarter? That time when my own revered parent, casting that significant "I know what you did" look at us, had dutifully defended us, using those fatal last words, "**My** children wouldn't do a thing like that" when his angry neighbor pointed to the tool box we kids had pilfered. How could Dad know? Besides, we did not steal anything. We thought we had been so clever. We hadn't broken the padlock. We had used Mama's little kitchen screwdriver to take the lock off. We tried out all the tools in the box. It was fun. We didn't damage the saw teeth **very** much. Then we put the tools back into the toolbox and screwed the undamaged lock back in place. Dad must have seen us running away after the fact.)

"After all, wild animals don't know any better," continued Homo Sap. "They have never had access to the knowledge of right and wrong. They don't know any better. Men do—or at least they should."

"Why are the wild animals so innocent?" I asked myself the same question I remembered asking my own father, when he'd said the same thing about the innocence of wild animals. I had argued that "they fight and kill each other. They even eat each other up!"

I almost blurted out the same answer to Homo Sap that I had come up with in those far too long ago days before my father could even proffer one up. With the brilliance of infancy I had immediately deduced and eagerly offered in my memory: Of course, Daddy, the poor creatures had to eat each other because they didn't know how to make soy burgers.

"Are you going to ask a question?" Not privy to my personal conversation Homo Sap watched a range of emotions pass across my face.

"I already have," I answered and left it at that.

Homo Sap just smiled, *just* like my father did, when I thought myself so clever and mysterious.

Leaving the Garden

I was dumfounded.

"You say God didn't drive Adam and Eve out of the Garden of Eden? Their own kinfolk did? Why?"

Homo Sap shrugged.

"They were–different," he said finally. "There were no others like them in the Garden of Eden, and the other animals called them freaks and monsters. The animals said that their mothers should have thrown them out to die when they were newborn."

"According to the *Bible*, God made Adam and Eve; they weren't born," I objected.

"Neither were the other animals. They were all created," Homo Sap agreed. "To make Adam, God took a gene here and a gene there from His pool, and when He combined them, Adam was not the same as His other creations. He had to create Eve because Adam was so lonely. Both were shunned by the rest of the creatures of His creation. The lesser animals, even those related to mankind, had forgotten their universal kinship as beings formed by the same Shaper. They looked at humans, so different from them and considered our First Ancestors to be incredibly ugly and deformed."

"I can't see why. Man looks pretty good to me."

"Especially the female version," Perky chimed in, popping up out of nowhere and to nowhere he seemed to disappear.

"Of course you can't! You are a human, too. But if you were a chimpanzee, you would feel differently. Think how you'd look to a chimp."

"How?"

"Well, you'd look as if your head were an outsize pumpkin, for one thing. Your legs would look like those of a daddy longlegs and your arms would seem almost as short—in their eyes—as those of a deformed wallaby. Hardly any body hair either, nearly bald all over, with no tusks or snout!"

"Ha! I think their arms are too long and their legs are too short—and they have no chins." I thrust mine out pugnaciously.

"I'm not taking sides," Homo Sap replied, "just telling you that Humans were not to the other animals' taste, and they wouldn't allow them in their territories. When their tribes observed Adam and Eve running away from God, they added to the hullabaloo so the freaked-out pair couldn't understand a word in the clatter and drove the two anomalies further and further away each day, until at last, Adam and Eve found themselves, not only outside but far, far distant from the gates of Eden."

"But what about the angel with the flaming sword," I protested. "Didn't he prevent them from re-entering Eden?"

"Oh, no," Homo Sap assured me. "He was really yelling at them to stop running, to come back, please do not run away, but they were so spooked when the other animals turned on them, they thought he was chasing them out, too."

"Their guilty consciences, I presume," I said sarcastically, "After all, they *had* eaten of the fruit of the Tree of Knowledge of good and evil without God's permission."

"That's right, but they were wrong about that, too, of course. God wanted them to have the Knowledge, but He wanted them to be developed enough to cope with it—to have the experience to evaluate it, first."

"Why?"

"Well, knowledge is like a knife. With it, you can slice a loaf of bread, or you can cut your fingers off."

"I know that," I agreed. "You've got to understand how to use any tool before you employ it," and muttered under my breath, "Any fool knows that."

"Usually after he's chopped off his fingers," Homo Sap countered. "To get on with our story, Adam and Eve took to the savannahs, their kinfolk behind them, pelting them with rocks. But when God finally got through to them, they were reluctant to go back to live with the other animals. Since that was what they wanted (I tell you, God really spoiled that boy, Adam!), he gave the children of Adam and Eve the same ability as the other creatures on Earth to physically adapt to their environment outside Eden. How else could they have survived in an alien environment? So mankind kept changing and changing."

"That's true. A couple million years ago, prehistoric man and his ancestors didn't look much like us." I granted.

"No, they didn't," Homo Sap agreed, "but, unfortunately, modern man still has at least one genetic trait in common with all the other lesser animals."

"What's that?" I asked suspiciously.

"If a human being encounters another human being the least bit different from himself, he will drive him away, ill-treat him, devour him or destroy his species."

"Nonsense," I protested, "nothing of the kind!"

"What about racism?" Homo Sap asked quietly. "What about the way little children treat each other and gang up on the one who is weaker or different in some way? What about our bullets, bayonets and nuclear bombs, or, for that matter, what about that serial killer in the Midwest United States, who devoured his victims or served them at dinner to his friends?"

I winced inwardly as I thought about how, as a child, I had been taunted as "four eyes" and "owl eyes", because I wore glasses, which magnified the size of my eyes. I remembered how some of the bigger children had seized my glasses one day and stomped on them just for fun; so I had to blindly grope my way home. (I was so traumatized that I was among the first to have laser eye surgery.) I recalled how no one played with poor little Billy anymore, because he had been crippled and disfigured by polio, how religious differences could lead to war and bloodshed.

"But we are God's highest creation," I protested feebly.

"Someday we may be," Homo Sap replied thoughtfully, "when He has completed us."

I was appalled. "Do you mean that you think we are still in the process of creation, that God has not finished making us?"

"You think Man is perfect as he is, do you?" Homo Sap asked in return.

I thought of man, supposedly civilized, killing, maiming, brutalizing, torturing his fellow men all over the globe–and in every case for the stupidest of reasons–and had to confess he *could* stand improvement.

"Since Time means nothing in Eternity," I opined, "I suppose you could say that God is still stirring the pot. But why didn't He make us go back to Eden when the other animals threw us out?"

"Because Man *is* God's highest creation. Having given us Reason, He gave us this world for a classroom. As we learn and change for the better, so we change our world. When we have become what God planned us to be, then our world itself will be an Eden."

"If we don't kill ourselves off, first," I said resignedly, thinking of the latest outbreaks of violent racism in almost every country on the globe.

"That is a possibility," Homo Sap agreed. "God gave us Free Will to make our own choices, too. How else can we learn?"

On Laziness

"Where is that photographer?" I muttered out loud, as I entered the Noble Savage's clearing, starting a recurring and sore subject with me. "Perky is nowhere about to take pictures."

"I am sure he is somewhere," the Noble Savage interrupted my thoughts. "Let's go look for him."

So, for about 2 hours I traipsed after Homo Sap and got completely exhausted, even though I had gotten myself into pretty good shape. We went around the village and then deep into the rain forest, the light around us turning from a golden to dusky green luminosity. On our return to the village after Sap's search, we came upon Perky, lying in a hammock with four women surrounding him. One was feeding him fruits from the jungle, one was fanning him with a huge leaf and another was washing his feet. The fourth, the woman we met named Silesia, was standing on the side, but her body language belied that she was not totally approving of these ministrations.

These women were not the older women with drooping, gravity-stretched breasts, but young and vivacious vixens. Like Homo Sap, they had complexions that ranged from golden to a warm chocolate. Their features were Romanesque with a touch of Aztec, but some also had larger lips and heavier bone structures. These beautiful women ranged through the racial prototypes, but their exact racial background was impossible to tell.

Their breasts, the size of ripe apples, bobbed pleasingly as they moved. Normally, I would turn myself away from this disgusting display of bouncing breasts, but the fourth woman seemed to glow a golden light and I could not take my eyes off her beauty. My normal, civilized moralistic judgments were distracted beyond recovery.

I was able compose myself with great difficulty and then ranted at Perky to cover my embarrassment. "How lazy can you be?"

"I have already taken 439 pictures of the flora and fauna," Perky defended himself. "I was just taking a break, but I have been workin', boss." Pulling out his camera, while laying in his hammock, Perky clicked the shutter and engulfed me in a blinding flash. "Now, I gotta take some more pictures of Flora and Fauna."

"Flora and Fauna?" I stuttered, but before I finished stuttering Perky was re-aiming the camera at two of the women, who were taking care of him. Then I realized that with a limited vocabulary Perky had just picked names out of the air for some of his new female friends. "And Kapuana, too"

"Don't forget Silesia," Homo Sap interjected with a smile. Even with my explosion at Perky, Homo Sap could not miss my inability to take my eyes off Silesia and craftily surmised what I could not or would not. Silesia sensed my eyes upon her. She went over to a nearby bush and picked a red rose. Handing me the rose, she smiled and then left.

I found Homo Sap staring at me, most amused by what had just occurred.

Jerking myself back to reality, I assessed the situation at hand. Perky had apparently been taking pictures, but I was not sure if it was the flora and fauna or Flora and Fauna. Totally exasperated, I followed Homo Sap back to his clearing with the hammock, fuming.

"That lazy good-for-nothing!" I expounded.

"I'm surprised at all this fuss about being lazy. Lazy is as Lazy does! We should be thanking God we can be lazy. Light has a shadow, every virtue a vice, and conversely every vice has a virtue. That's what civilization is all about. Roads, tools, art, houses, cars, everything man has, results from man's directed sloth. Ever since man got up on two feet, a desire to take his ease has been his motive for creating lots more time to loaf and dream. The only catch is that the more free time he makes for himself, the more widely educated he needs to be in order to fill up the empty hours. It's hard work trying to avoid the boredom of having nothing to do, much harder than working on a job you don't like! A million or so years ago, a primitive Homo sap got tired of running from palm to palm waiting for coconuts to fall on a rock and break open so he could eat them." Homo Sap espoused. "Too much work! My ancestor must have grumbled that there must be an easier way."

"Being lazy is being productive?" I still had a hard time looking away from Silesia.

"You are a civilized man, correct?"

"Of course!"

"I am just a lowly savage," Homo Sap deferred to my superior wisdom, which I liked, or was he deferring to my unbounded egotism, which thought I could not intellectually accept. "But I can envisage my ancestor, loafing in the sun eating coconut meat, when he saw a rock lying near a fallen coconut. Hmm, he thought, instead of waiting for the coconut to fall on the rock and break open so he could eat the meat, why not hit the coconut with the rock? He tried it out. It worked. He had so much more time to do what he liked between meals he wondered what else would make life easier and invented a fish spear."

"Now my ancestor Sap lay round most of the time, his friends jeering at his sloth while they worked around the clock looking for coconuts, which occasionally broke as they fell from the tree."

"You've got no work ethic," they said.

"Sure haven't!" he replied with a happy grin. "I only work to LIVE; you live to WORK. In fact, if your civilization cut the working week down to 4 days without pay reduction and hired extra help at time and a half, your society's economy would skyrocket overnight and would have to double the size and number of arenas for the expanded recreational needs of people without a creative bent."

"Not everyone is a genius, my ancestor Sap would have said modestly when asked how he thought up all these great notions, Not everyone can figger out ways to do so little and enjoy so much more free time, so I fill up my extra loafing time thinking of fun ideas for them, because I've been told there is a feller down there who has some mischief still for folks that don't know what to do with their idle hands."

"Someday when folks learn to be really lazy and like it, learn to make laziness happily productive for EVERYONE, not just themselves, they will make androids to press the buttons for us, while we play golf or tinker with our chemistry kits." Sap said.

"Working is a matter of perception. Some people say I work too much," Homo Sap grinned. "They're wrong. Just because they don't find fun in the same things, they think I'm working. They have the wrong definition of work. If you do it because you must, even if you hate the job or product, because you have to eat and pay the rent, that's work. It stands to reason those workers will get depressed, restless, inattentive, tired, dawdle and quit early. On a job they enjoy, you'll have to drag them away to eat or sleep. That's play. That's fun. That's genuine laziness putting fantasy into action. That's the kind of laziness I'm enjoying. My work is my leisure, my pleasure, my fun."

I was just dumbstruck at this line of logic. I understood then just how savage this man really was and, conversely, how civilized I was. I thought to myself: "Work has to be work and play has to be play. Now that is being enlightened!"

"Besides," the Noble Savage chuckled devilishly. "Laziness is the virtue of philosophers and the bane of dictators. Tyrants can't do *anything* if their lazy people won't do *something*. Ghandi proved that.")

Women in Battle

"Life here cannot be ideal. You must have had trouble from neighboring tribes." I asked.

"Once, the Lluhters invaded out territory." Homo Sap admitted.

"When the Lluhters descended like the wolf on the fold, Homo Sap, what did your tribe do?"

"We did the best we could," he replied simply.

"With so few in your tribe, however did you manage to defeat them?" I was in awe of this accomplishment; I also marveled at the fact that Perky had deigned to show up for this interview.

"We used every available body in the tribe to repel them."

"Even women?"

"Even women," was the grim rejoinder.

"But women are so slight, so frail," Perky objected. "Weren't they a hazard in hand-to-hand battle?"

"No more than anybody else. After all, some men are very small and weak, not much use in battle. We employ them as runners or clerks. We need them as much as we need warriors. Same with women; if they had the physique to withstand the trials of combat, we used them on the front line. If they didn't, we had them as a backup."

"Back-up?" We repeated.

"Yes, a back-up. When the enemy is breathing in your face, you welcome anybody at your side that can give support. Man or woman, it makes no difference. A two-handed sword is a powerful engine of destruction, but it's heavy as hell. So we issued neat, small stilettos to the women. This made them equal on the line. Now YOU have a rifle–that makes your men

39

and women even more equal. Doesn't take the strength of an ox to pull a trigger!"

"But don't women panic and become hysterical in battle? Won't that ruin the morale of the troops, causing them to lose their cool—and maybe the battle—under fire?"

"No more than men, and not if the women are well trained. If your troops are falling apart in battle, sack your trainer. Good training makes for good morale and coolness under fire."

"Maybe we're prejudiced about women being in battle."

"I am, too," said Homo Sap dryly. "Shows me that tribal order has broken down, and we're on the way to the Dark Ages again."

"Why?" I asked curiously. I could see no connection between women in battle and the Dark Ages.

"Women probably started civilization when they put plants in the ground, kept chickens or ducks in a pen and started making rules like, 'Don't track mud in the house', 'wash your hands', and 'no fighting at the dinner table or in the yard. You crushed my tomatoes in your last battle; above all, **don't kill your brother!**' So you see, when women are as eager to kill as men, they are no longer civilizers; they have become as savage as men."

"But women want to be equal."

"Equal in what? Killing? Brutality? They used to leave the blood and gore to their men, the brutes."

"But to stand beside your man in battle—is that too much to ask?"

"You know what they say. If you can't lick them, join them. If your women can't humanize you, I suppose there's nothing else for them to do except join the men when they play war games."

"I suppose you don't want women in battle with you either," I said offended.

Homo Sap laughed. "I didn't say that at all! I don't even want an army. I said that **if** we are attacked, I don't care who is protecting my rear, or my front, as long as I don't get killed! Man or woman, makes no difference to me, but I always thought women were too smart to kill anything except a chicken for dinner."

Harassment

After a long walk around the forest looking for indigenous food stuffs, we struggled into camp, hot and thirsty; it was annoying to see Homo Sap taking his ease in a hammock and plucking an occasional grape from an overhanging vine.

"You look disturbed," he remarked after swallowing the purple goody. He pulled down a bunch and tossed it over.

I caught it deftly.

"Refresh yourself with these berries." he invited. "Grab a hammock, get off those sore feet and do some quality thinking."

"Thanks! You'd be hurting if you were in my shoes."

Homo Sap looked at his bare toes.

"I would," he agreed smugly.

I pulled grapes one-by-one from the stem, while handing a second bunch to Perky, my lazy photographer, who ate a few before settling down for a snooze. One of the beautiful women he gallivanted with appeared and fanned him with a wet palm leaf.

"I'm being sued for sexual harassment."

"If you harassed someone, why not? You know the law in the United States. Dare I ask which sex?"

"Female, of course. I'm a heterosexual male, dammit!"

"A heterosexual male usually harasses females," he agreed, "but not always. You might have been a bisexual, harassing other males. How would I know?"

"Never! You know I'm not gay," I protested.

"I know now," he admitted, recalling a recent episode observing my behavior in the presence of Silesia. "Before, I only surmised. You don't look joyous."

"You should have known," I replied grumpily. "Have I ever looked at you like one of those?"

"Oh, there's a way to tell the difference? I thought you had to ask to find out—or they had to tell."

"Of course they look like everybody else, the unnatural monsters!"

"If they look like everybody else, then we all look like unnatural monsters," Homo Sap pointed out. "You aren't making yourself clear."

"How can I be, with you confusing me all the time? I told you, my newspaper is dealing with a multi-million dollar civil suit for sexual harassment. Just because I'm a heterosexual male, they act as if I'm out to rape every woman I see. And I'm not!"

"Ah!" Homo Sap nodded wisely, "You approached a lesbian with a proposition; she repulsed you because you weren't her sexual preference."

"No, no, no! I hate gays. I don't want them near me, male or female!"

"But how can you avoid them if they don't wear a sign? Your best friend may be gay."

"Impossible," I replied. "Alex is a macho man. He pulled me out of a burning car once. You wouldn't believe his courage. He..."

"Oh, I would," Homo Sap cut me off hurriedly. "He could be all those things and still be gay. Would you give up his friendship if he is?"

I thought about it. "Alex, a gay? Suppose he was? Could I throw away someone who had saved my life?"

"No, no! Alex is a man's man!" I protested.

"Male gays are," Homo Sap agreed.

I shuddered. "You may be right. There ought to be some way to tell which sheep is really a wolf."

"For that matter," Sap added thoughtfully, "how can gays find each other without a sign? They must be mighty lonesome people."

"How can you talk like that?" I was appalled. "I don't care if they ever find each other as long as they don't find ME!"

"Are you sure you are not gay?" Homo Sap scratched his head. "You're acting so defensively, it makes me think you are."

"Argh!" I sputtered.

"Ah, I gather then, you found a heterosexual female to harass!"

"I didn't harass her! I was trying to date her."

"So you could sexually harass her?" Homo Sap questioned.

"Look, Sap, this is no joke. This suit may cost my newspaper a bundle of money and sink me professionally; it may have been one of the reasons why the editor agreed so quickly to send me out of the country. All this because I touched her–er–shoulder flirtatiously. She looked so luscious in that sexy off-the-shoulder blouse. I thought she was looking for–er–willing to—" I choked on a grape. Sap thumped my back and finished the sentence for me.

"Take an adult, man-with-woman, roll in the hay with you?"

"Yes–no–that is, I was only trying to be friendly. She misunderstood the whole thing." I was becoming frustrated. "Heck, when she said no, I left her alone, but she must have thought she could make some quick money through litigation."

"Calm down," Sap advised. "It's only a misunderstanding! Explain it to the judge, and you'll be cleared of guilt."

"Not these days! Man, you don't know how lucky you are to be living in the jungle. It's a sexual witch-hunt back there with males as the persecuted witches. A heterosexual man only has to look crosswise at a woman, and he's in the meat-house for harassment or rape–even if she deliberately lured me on with her slinky walk and bare shoulder."

"You think it was deliberate? You were able to read her mind?" Sap probed.

"No."

"Could she read yours?"

"No." Thank God for that, I thought.

"Then maybe she really believed you had evil intentions."

"Hell, no! Not me."

"Seems to me," Sap drawled judiciously, "your society needs some good, old-fashioned courtship rituals–you know, manners and rules designed to let a girl know what you mean, and let you know when she means no, even if she's only wearing a bikini bottom."

"Mating rites? *How savage!*" I ejaculated. "I know how to court a girl."

"Do you?" Homo Sap asked dryly. "If so, why have you hired a lawyer?"

I dropped my head dejectedly. "I was misunderstood."

"Probably," Homo Sap responded. "Men and women don't speak the same language. Indeed, sometimes I don't think they belong to the same species. A woman shrugs her shoulders. A man sees an invitation. She slaps his face. He doesn't know why. She only shrugged her shoulders. On the other hand, he said he'd give her a ring. She sues him for breach of promise because he told her he'd marry her. He protests he only said he'd phone her."

"True!" I gasped.

"That's why you need a social code or language. We use the language of flowers. For instance, a white rose in a girl's hair, or in your case, perhaps, on her desk, means don't touch! I'm holding out for marriage. A red carnation, on the other hand, means not on the job! See me after work. A purple tulip signifies I'm gay. Are you? An orange lily is a warning sign, indicating that I'm willing, but when was your last AIDS check-up? You see? No mistakes and no one is lonely."

"That's fine for you, but in the meantime, what shall I do?"

"There's a way around everything. Go Platonic! Give her a sigh, not the eye."

"What does a red rose mean?" I asked, recalling what Silesia had given to me.

"A red rose? It means," the Noble Savage smiled, somewhat savagely I thought. "I love you, you idiot!"

The Hold-up Man

We were strolling with Homo Sap around a neighboring village. The villagers did not look happy to see us. I shivered under their furtive glares. Their heavy brow ridges looked threatening, their large sharp teeth ominous, but the sight of the human finger bones waggling like white moustaches in the cartilage of their noses was horrifying. My young cameraman cowered against me nervously.

"How did they get the finger bones? Did they cut the fingers off cadavers?" Perky whispered and then speculated loudly. "Or cut off the hand of their much alive victims?"

I rolled my eyes and looked inquiringly at Homo Sap.

"The Lhuters are armed robbers, not professional killers. Hold-up men, I think you'd call them." Homo Sap shrugged as he strolled besides me. "When they are hungry or desperate, they attack people from richer tribes and steal their seashells, their clothes, their food or their smaller body parts. If the victim resists, a hold-up man stuns his victim with his throwing stone or his hammer stone. Sometimes the victim dies."

"I'd keep my own throwing stone handy," I averred valiantly, "and I'd throw to kill if attacked. Wouldn't you?"

"Not the best answer," said Homo Sap. "A Lhuter always has his stone at hand. He has the element of surprise. By the time you fumbled your stone out of your breech cloth, he would have cracked your skull and begun to gnaw off your fingers."

"You don't stone them back?" My assistant and I gasped in shock. "You don't knock their skulls in?"

"Too much work," Homo Sap yawned.

"What do you do?"

"Talk."

"Talk? TALK!"

"The tongue is mightier than the stone–or the gun."

"Impossible. I wouldn't dare to go out in Texas without my six shooter," I blurted. "I'll blow away any mugger to Kingdom Come."

"If he–or his accomplice–doesn't get you first from behind."

"You've just never had to face a real hold-up Lhuter or gunman," I challenged Homo Sap.

"Indeed I have."

"What happened?"

"I talked him out of it.[2] In fact, by the time I had finished telling him my pitiful tale of poverty and grief; he sobbed on my shoulder and gave me all the shells in his pouch."

"Why shells?" I asked, puzzled. "What good are shells?"

"Shells are money in these parts," Homo Sap dryly replied. "He thought money would solve his problems."

---

2   This story, "The Hold-up Man", is based on truth. Somewhere between 1919/21, an armed robber held up my father, Andrew J. MacDonnell. My dad held up his arms. "Take anything I have," he said, "I know you must be in worse need than I, to take to robbery."

His attitude astonished the thief, and they pursued a brief conversation in which each revealed his problems. In the end, the thief handed back my father's money. My father refused to take it all back.

"I know you are down on your luck or you wouldn't be here. Take enough to get a start on something better. Try for a job in the factory. Tell them Andy sent you."

The would-be thief went away weeping. The event left a definite impression on me that weapons are no safeguards but rather a provocation to violence. Some years later, a sporty red car drove into our isolated farmyard. A handsome, well-dressed young man got out and helped a pretty young lady out to stand beside him. The noise of the engine brought dad out into the sunshine. "Remember me, Andy?" He cried out joyfully. "I'm Al Munoz, and this is my bride to be." Then he turned to us and said, "Did your dad ever tell you how I tried to rob him once, because I was down and out? Did he tell you how he saved MY life in a way and started me on the path to happiness and good fortune?" Then he told us the story, which became the inspiration for "The Hold-up man".

By the way, when he was about 81, (he only claimed 'going on to about 78') my father was cited in the Chester Times, for foiling a robbery by his tackling–himself unarmed–an armed thief. N.M.Barraford.

The Weapons-makers

I had barely put my knapsack down when a panting, almost naked messenger hurtled out of the perfumed, tropical night into Homo Sap's presence. In his haste, he almost fell over my cameraman, relaxing near the communal fire. The draft as he ran by the fire blew the flames and smoke into the Elders' eyes. They coughed and snorted in disgust.

"Haste makes waste," they muttered, as the gasping messenger came to a dead stop.

Homo Sap threw his legs over the side of his hammock and sat up. "Catch your breath, son," he said mildly. "I presume you have important news."

"Yes, yes," the messenger panted. "The Yuks and Yohs are killing each other."

"What for?" I asked, while Homo Sap was pondering this news.

"They don't like each other, never have, for at least a thousand years." Sap responded to my question and then to the messenger he said: "Are the Universal Peacemen aware of this uprising?"

"Yes, but the Yuks and Yohs are threatening to kill the unarmed Peacemen."

"Um! They must be stopped," Homo Sap agreed. Then he frowned. "You say they are killing each other? What are they killing each other with?"

"They have swords, spears and guns."

"Ah! Then our elders shall soon put matters to rights," Homo Sap said. "Go light the signal fire for all the elders from every tribe to gather here in council."

As the messenger, still breathless with excitement, rushed off to light the signal fire, I asked Homo Sap what was happening. I looked back over my shoulder nervously; the jungle night seemed suddenly menacing.

"War has broken out between two factions in one of the local tribes," he replied briefly.

"Is it very serious? Will it be safe to stay here? Or should we leave before war spreads to your tribe?"

"No, no," Homo Sap replied easily. "We shall extinguish this small conflagration. Its flames shall not scorch you, although many in that tribe may suffer injury and death, alas, before the war is over."

"You say that the council will soon put matters to rights," I said. "Are you going to teach them a lesson by crushing them with your superior numbers and weaponry? Show them who's boss with death and mayhem?"

"Oh, no," Homo Sap replied, shocked. "Nothing like that!"

"Then how will the council stop them?" I demanded.

"Very simple. We shall have to find the weapons-maker who is supplying the rebellious forces with arms and tell him that the Yuks and the Yohs may not have further ordinance until they have made peace."

"And that will stop the war?" I asked incredulously. "Won't the rebels make their own weapons?"

"If they could make enough of their own weapons, they wouldn't be buying any."

"But they're poor. Where do they get the money for their guns?"

"By impoverishing themselves even more. You can't have guns *and* butter."

"So they will still fight each other."

"True, but with less ammunition, they will find it harder to conduct a war, and we'll find it easier to contain it," Homo Sap replied. "Fists and stones are easier to avoid than bullets."

"But will your weapons-makers listen?" I asked cynically, remembering the international German and American cartel of armament makers in WWI, who helped each other fill orders for BOTH sides, uncaring whether their bullets killed their own or the opposition's soldiers. Even today, there is still a lot of gun smuggling to South America, Iran, Ireland. "From my knowledge of the breed, the weapons-makers would only see a ban on arms as an easy new way to make bigger–and untaxed–profits."

"I'm sure you are right," Homo Sap agreeably assented, "So we don't ban weapons."

"What do you do?"

Homo Sap grinned.

"We hit them in the pocketbook."

"How?" I marveled.

"Every weapon bears the thumbprint of its maker. In peace or war, if even one is found in the hands of the Yuks or the Yohs, we impose a fine so heavy on that gun firm it makes such deals highly unprofitable for them. We don't accept excuses for the presence of their weapons among the Yuks and the Yohs, either. We don't even ask how the weapons got there. We just make the cost of illegal arms so expensive, that they must obey the laws or lose their businesses. We don't put them in jail, either. Keeping them in jails is too expensive. We just take away most of the weapons-makers' money and make selling armaments so unprofitable they close up shop. Anyone, caught making arms, has to give them over to the chief and pay a heavy fine as well. Melting the weapons down and turning them into fish hooks and frying pans is much more rewarding."

On Fanaticism

The muted green-gold light of the jungle was soothing after the hot glare of sun on sand. Gratefully we fanned ourselves with our sun hats as we hurried on our way through the aisles of tall trees and trailing vines. As Perky and I expected, Homo Sap was relaxing lazily in one of the hammocks of split and woven liana, each strung between the giant trees.

"Hi, boys," he greeted us, genially. "Grab a hammock and rest a spell."

We sat down with sighs of pleasure.

"Just a little idea that came to me when I was watching an oriole build her nest," Homo Sap said, indicating the hammocks. "Have you noticed they're not only comfortable for lying in, but if you push gently with your foot and swing, they cause a cooling breeze?"

"Yes, yes, Sap," we said impatiently, "but we have important news!"

"I thought as much," Homo Sap sighed. "What is it this time?"

"The Yuks and the Yohs are still at it. Since you have successfully stopped the flow of weapons, we wanted to see if they'd any weapons stockpiled. So we had rowed down the river to where there was a break in the rainforest canopy to their beachhead, when they attacked us. We raced away as fast as we could, but before we were out of ear-shot they said that they'd fight us to the death of every man, woman and child."

"What did you do?"

"Rowed faster! The crazy bastards yelled non-stop, irrationally."

"Of course, do you think fighting is rational conduct?"

"I think they think they are rational and ready to defend their tribe for a good cause."

"Defense is the opposite of attack—" He muttered off-handedly to himself, then addressed himself to me, "Their cause is not a good cause?"

"Of course not! The Yohs insist that their crazy God is better than the Yuks or even ours. It's enough to make any Patriot's blood boil. By God, we'll show them they can't insult our God or country." (Looking back on this conversation, I realize that maybe I was going 'native' faster than expected. The problem is that I was not sure if I was talking about Yu, the God of the Yuks, or Yo, the God of the Yohs or my God, whichever one that was.)

"YOUR God? I thought there is only one God."

"There IS only one God–OURS, and we'll die before we'll let those Yuks—ah, Yohs—bad mouth HIM."

"You say *you* are not a fanatic?"

"Of course not! We're just good old-fashioned patriots, willing to DIE FOR GOD AND COUNTRY. Anytime. OUR GOD OR COUNTRY, RIGHT OR WRONG!" I noted with satisfaction. "At the moment, they are trapped. They can't get out, but when we get them out, we'll show those Yoyos what's right from wrong."

"How?"

"We'll imprison them in a loony bin, or jail, and take their children away from them."

Homo Sap looked thoughtfully at us. "You want to imprison them?"

"Yes."

Homo Sap sighed and again I saw the flicker of sadness pass across his eyes.

"And you say they can't get out of their *compongs*?" Homo Sap asked me this question, patiently, as if asking a child.

"Correct."

"Are their weapons depleted?"

"We saw nothing on our foray," I stated. "All they could do was to throw sticks and stones at us."

"Why worry then? They are already imprisoned in a mutual jail of their own choosing. Keep them there."

I was shocked.

"But they mocked us. How will we get even? We've got to show them they can't flout the law!"

Homo Sap looked at us compassionately. "Can you reason with them?"

"No, they won't act in a rational manner."

"Does it matter what a madman thinks as long as he is confined and can't or won't come out to hurt you?"

As usual, Homo Sap's twisted view of reality tied my tongue for a moment.

"You don't take anything seriously," I said in hurt tones.

"I take fanaticism very seriously," Homo Sap replied. "Fanatic adherence to ideas and principles has built many civilizations. It has also torn them down. When fanatics fight and die for the right groups against the right enemies, we call them heroes, no matter how many innocents die with them. People will kill themselves or ask their friends to kill them for fear of falling into enemy hands and giving away vital information under torture."

"Of course! Patriotic women have even killed their children and themselves to prevent ignoble enslavement by the enemy. Death before Dishonor! Live free or die! Give me liberty or give me death!" I agreed smugly.

"Is dying for a good cause to help others reasonable, or is it a sign of insanity to consider dying for any cause?" Homo Sap asked whimsically. "After all, fanaticism is only a stubborn adherence to a particular point of view, which the fanatic thinks is good."

Confused, I rose and turned to leave for my *compong*. Perky followed reluctantly, his eyes longingly meeting those of a delectable maiden.

"Maybe we'd better start building insane asylums instead of jails," I added sarcastically, "Since it seems even patriots appear to be as sick as serial killers."

Homo Sap grinned. "Yep, that might be the answer. To prevent crime, we've tried beating, torture and capital punishment with no success for thousands of years. Violent criminals don't seem to mind dying by gun, gas, hanging, guillotine or electric chair. I wonder how they would feel about a lifetime as psychiatric guinea pigs. Shock therapy is electrifying, I'm told, and water therapy downright chilly."

"Are you serious?"

"Aren't you? Like Fanatics, most criminals are motivated by poverty, ignorance or mental illness, whether hereditary or induced by stressful circumstances. TREATMENT might be a BETTER and CHEAPER deterrent of fanaticism or crime THAN PUNISHMENT."

Why Trees?

When Homo Sap was asked what he thought about the destruction of the forests to supply lawyers with all the paper they use every month–about 130 tons a firm–he lazily shrugged his shoulders and said, "There must be an easier way to make paper and save SOME trees. Think of all those loggers grunting and groaning as they chop down mango trees to make into paper; all that sweat–and sometimes blood, if a log rolls over and smooches one of us primates. Ugh!"

"But tree cutting makes jobs," Perky protested, "I worked with a lumber crew during one of my college breaks. That's how I could afford to buy this super camera." He drew his hand reverently over its lens.

"Sure–as long as there are some trees left to cut. Still, when the trees go, so will those jobs–as well as the spotted owl. Not that I mind the owl so much. It's tough and stringy eating–only one or two bites on its bones–, and hardly worth catching. But the deer and the turkey will go with the owl. If they go, we go hungry."

Homo Sap was asked what he'd do about replacing the wood pulp needed for paper if the forests were to be left undisturbed.

"As I pointed out to our EC, Environmental Chief to you," Homo Sap remarked loftily then deflated noticeably. "Sorry, I got carried away with the civilized habit of creating titles for people and making acronyms out of their titles, but it is the lazy thing to do, which hearkens to my savage nature."

"EC sounds like one of the bird calls around here," Perky illuminated us with his vast knowledge, and then to our startled sensibilities he mimicked the birds, screaming. "EC, EC!"

I could have sworn that in the distance I heard an answering call.

3   Lawyers need paper by the ton, they say, according to a TV comment on 6/10/92.

"Well, cotton is cellulose, too." Homo Sap continued, ignoring Perky's stab at imitating bird calls.

"Cellulose?" Perky asked with a puzzled frown. "Isn't that something cows eat?" (Honestly! Don't they teach these kids anything in college today?)

"Sure is," Homo Sap replied, "but it makes great paper, too. Our lawyers might prefer paper made from cotton–or flax–because it lasts longer than wood paper. Why cotton and linen mummy wrappings have lasted thousands of years. Gives a man a good feeling to know posterity will be able to see what a good job he did!"

"Then why are we using up trees?" Perky was puzzled.

"Beats me! I guess it seemed the cheapest way to go when we thought forests were expendable. We know better now. Why some of those giant sequoias took thousands of years to grow! In one lifetime, who can replace them? Cotton is different. You can grow fresh plants every year, and we have a lot of marginal soil where more and more cotton can be grown with a little fertilizer and a lot of effort."

"But what about the out-of-work loggers?" I wailed.

"Didn't I say effort?" Homo Sap queried. "Train them on the machines and set them to work harvesting and processing the cotton. It takes less toil than logging, and, although there's a lot of sweat involved, there's a lot less blood and tears."

He sniffed the resinous breeze gently stirring the boughs of the forest primeval about him.

"So your tribe stopped logging intensively?" I pursed my lips.

Homo Sap waved his arm amiably. "We sure did. See that virgin forest? What's good for the spotted owl is just as good for us. Those aren't tulips standing about as hammock holders."

Perky shivered as the trees rustled menacingly, murmuring sly commentaries about him. "Aren't you afraid trees might take over the world?"

"Take over the world? You've lived in the city too long, if you are paranoid about trees." Homo Sap scoffed. "Don't you know that while people can live almost anywhere, trees, that supply us with much of the oxygen we need to survive, can't? The world doesn't have many green belts. Most of the Earth is ice, ocean, mountain, or desert, which won't support any tree giants. But, by symbiosis, cotton and man can turn semi-arable lands into very productive areas. Animal wastes can supply the soil with the necessary nitrogen to make cotton a lush producer. Caring for the cotton, picking and processing, it can provide jobs and money for out of work loggers–or even farmers. As I suggested to our 'EC'," he grinned at me slyly, "we had a lot of semi-desert land lying fallow near the mountains, which could be used for growing cotton. Recognizing a great idea when he heard it, he told the tribe to put down their axes, grab shovels and grow cotton for cloth and paper."

He paused for effect–Homo Sap is a real emoter! "So we grow cotton and even flax for linen paper. Now we have all the paper we want and can use the cotton and flax seeds for oil and cattle fodder as well, while the money we get from our scribes–lawyers to you–for our paper keeps us all in the best bananas and coconut milk."

Perky was impressed.

"Why, using cotton for paper could revive the entire south," Perky marveled, "and provide more jobs than the tobacco companies. Think of all the jobs the cotton industry would create, making paper for lawyers, not to mention newsprint, if they took over all those tobacco fields."

"Permanent jobs, too," Homo Sap pointed out complacently. "Scribes and lawyers are forever, and papers come out daily."

"So the rain forests could be saved for posterity?" Perky marveled.

"If they aren't saved, we may not have any posterity," Homo Sap pointed out dryly. "Alter the world too much, and our own species may find themselves unable to live on it."

When I finally got that lazy college boy back to work with his precious camera, making images of the forest primeval, Homo Sap was once more enjoying his favorite pastime, loafing under a tree, his head pillowed on a bag of cowrie shells, drowsily muttering something about contemplating further refinements for man's future. Cowrie shell pocket money was heavy to carry and hard to break up into even pieces for change. Perhaps paper money? Naw! That wore out too easily. Perhaps a mix of cotton or linen with silk spun by spiders or moths might make a washable paper for the mint, he muttered.

Trouble is, I muttered sarcastically, most of the primates in Homo Sap's tribe would likely prefer spider and moth larvae, not as paper makers, but as delectable hors d'oeuvres at a jungle feast.

Leaving The Jungle

Three months had passed quickly. I was looking over my notes and although money was not an issue, the loyalty I had for my editor urged me to collect my papers and go home to turn them in. There was a great feeling of sadness that I was leaving this place, but my concern for Perky was growing every day as he was going native on me. He had discarded his Western-type clothing months ago. (I was still in my Western clothes but the urge to slough them off was pulling at me constantly. Was I going because of Perky or because I was on the verge of going native myself?)

"Homo Sap," I announced as I pulled my backpack into his clearing. Perky forlornly followed me, awkwardly dressed again in Western clothes. (Why did we look so uncomfortable, when we were properly dressed?) "We are leaving the jungle."

"Is there any particular reason why?" Homo Sap got up from his hammock.

"Well, we came here to report your story and we have enough material now to do that," I explained. "In addition, Perky here has been out of film for a month. He has nothing to do." (Yes, this happened during those by-gone days when cameras used film.)

"Yes, but the reason I allowed you to come is still valid." Homo Sap agreed. "People need to look at the world, their country and themselves from different perspectives and I believe I have a different perspective, even though I am not modern by your standards."

"I do want to thank you for your help during this visit, it was wonderful, and I want to apologize for Perky here and his outlandish behavior among your young women." I did not want to bring up the touchy subject that one or two of them might be pregnant.

"There is nothing to apologize about," Homo Sap began.

"Yes there is," I interrupted. "He took advantage of those poor young ladies."

"Norman," Homo Sap addressed me by my name when he wanted to get my attention. "One could look at it from that perspective, but I could also say that our young women took advantage of Perky."

"How can you say that?" I was shocked, my Puritanical moral fabric horrified.

"When you are part of a small immobile group of people, intermarriage is inevitable causing the problems of inbreeding." Homo Sap remarked with a smile. "Whenever a new genetic source makes itself available, the temptation to inculcate it into our genetic pool can literally be a life-saver. Why do you think some of those island people in the South Pacific welcomed sailors so enthusiastically with open arms, literally? I personally think that some women are more sensitive than others to this genetic conundrum, which shows up in their sense of attraction. When new talent like you and Perky show up, the genetic magnetism is so irresistible, they can't help themselves."

"But some of those girls may, er, be…"

"Be pregnant." Homo Sap completed my sentence. "That is the whole point. I am sure the girls would be delighted and our tribe would welcome the additions, if they do come, not to mention refreshing the tribe's genetic material. We do not worry about any particular moral order by which children should come, only that they come to a mother that wants them and will love them. Having a father around is gravy, but children have grown up without fathers before."

"You are definitely savages," I declared.

"We are savages because we want to bring children into the world to be loved?"

"People should be married before they have children," I huffed.

"Even in your own world this is a view point that is being stretched with the acceptance of unmarried women having children, but that is not really the point here." Homo Sap paused thoughtfully. "Let me ask you whether a woman who is forced to have a baby will be more or less happy than a woman who willingly pursues having a baby."

"I would think she would be less happy," I countered, reluctantly.

"Does the woman who is unhappy," Homo Sap questioned, "have the best attitude toward the child, when it is born?"

"No, but she can learn to love the baby," I argued.

"That can happen," Homo Sap admitted. "But isn't it better for the woman and the child to wait until the woman is ready? Wouldn't your society be better off, if every woman that bore a child wanted to have him or her so they could love them?"

"Sorry," I wanted to be polite and leave on good terms, but this conversation was not going in a rational direction from my civilized perspective. "Sometimes women must have children, whether they want them or not. And they can be forced to love them afterwards."

"I admit that I am just a savage," Homo Sap steered our conversation away from this sensitive subject. "But we diverged from why you came here."

I nodded in silence as I listened to the words that I had just spoken. I was almost as shocked about what I had said as I was with Homo Sap's views on the subject. With one grand statement, I doomed a significant percentage of all future women to a fate of anger and drudgery.

"Let me take you to the river," he said.

Perky was unusually quiet. I am sure that there was a part of him that wanted to stay, a large part, but I held the fort for both of us. I, too, was quiet; unhappy that our farewell had not occurred more gracefully.

"I know Perky has been getting to know some women of our tribe very well," Homo Sap started up the conversation as they were closing in on the river. "But you know you have an admirer in Silesia."

"No," I instantly flushed with shame and excitement. Of course I knew about Silesia, but I had not given in to temptation. (Was this the real reason I was so desperate to leave now? Was this the dreaded (by women) Commitment Anxiety Syndrome? A hybrid condition between grief and anxiety, the major symptoms for this disorder are denial, autonomic hyperactivity (shortness of breath, dizziness, palpatations), vigilance (fight or flight) and avoidance. I was unwilling to ask that question of myself, possibly terrified by the answer.)

Homo Sap broke a long twig off a sapling and stirred the water in the river as one would stir a cup of coffee after putting in two cubes of sugar. I looked at Homo Sap as if he was crazy, which is probably what I thought he was, but would not admit it.

"What are you doing?"

"Thought I'd stir things up." Homo Sap replied with an enigmatic smile. "Just preparing the way for you; remember, rivers change constantly and never lead to the same place. If you ever want to find me again, you will have to come up the Orinoco, but this little magic stir should send you down a river that will get you closer to home. I have provided you a canoe, but you will not need a guide, and when you are done with the canoe leave it on the bank. The canoe will find its way home afterwards."

"Do you really think your magic works? Stirring the water will not make any difference." I stated my superior civilized perspective. (Perky later said I sounded arrogant and sarcastic. I countered that I was just being realistic.)

"If you ever come back," Homo Sap ignored my lack of manners, beaming with good humor. "Why don't you tell me if my stir worked?"

With final good-byes, we were off. The travel for the first couple of days went as planned without incident. Soon the dark canopy of the forest began to spread open.

"I know we are rowing downstream with the current, but leaving the jungle seems to have passed a little faster than I expected." I remarked to Perky, but he was still sulking about having left the girls in Homo Sap's tribe behind.

After another two days to my surprise, we were completely out of the jungle. Hard wood trees lined the banks and paths started to show up.

"Perky, it took us over a month to get in to find Homo Sap," I shook my head in disbelief. "It seems we are completely out of the forest in a week."

"I thought the river gets wider as we get closer to the ocean, but this estuary seems to be getting small." Perky noted, even his curiosity was being piqued. "Why don't we stop to scout around?"

"Good idea," I agreed.

After bringing the boat ashore at an area that led to a particularly large path, we followed the path for about half a mile.

"I could swear I heard a car horn," I looked at Perky and he looked back.

"I heard it too," He returned.

Within another hundred yards we climbed out of a ditch onto an asphalt highway. Up the road, not two hundreds yards away, we came across a bridge and on one side was a prominent sign that said "Welcome to Sherborn."

"We're in Massachusetts!" I announced, totally astounded.

"That was quite a stir," Perky piped up.

The Little Lame Boy and His Grandmother[4]

Two years had passed since we went to the jungle and conversed with Homo Sap and returned. We had left him ages ago in the depths of a rain forest; he and his tribe remained uncorrupted by the institutions of civilized folk that have changed the rest of us into immoral–or is that moral–monsters. Somehow, he knew all the answers.

The articles were published to great acclaim, giving me quite a reputation, but left me short of both the fame and fortune I desired. As the Noble Savage foretold, my sense of happiness was not yet sated. Perky went back to college and finished his bachelor's degree. After this period of time, Perky and I got together and discovered that our re-assimilation into modern society had not gone as smoothly as we had expected. The modern adage that happiness follows success is not always true. Perky and I were not as happy as we had been in the rain forest. In fact, we were not happy at all.

Even though I received some respectful comments from the anthropology cognoscenti, I realized that I was a better reporter than I was an anthropologist. I got back into the humdrum of reporting, births, deaths, politics. I puttered along, but I was thoroughly dissatisfied with what I was writing. In the United States, are we not supposed to represent a "modern" society of "modern" men and women? If we are so "modern", why do we have such savage news to report? If "modern" man was so advanced why did the "modern" nations of the world have to resort to violence to resolve their

---

4   A true story from 1929-30.

differences? My newspaper constantly reported how we did not follow the path of reason, causing me great tribulations.

Perky came back to the United States a changed man. The women that he used to gallivant with did not seem that interesting to him anymore and the new women he met, although charming, could not seem to comprehend his new depth of character. By the way, Perky no longer looked at women as playthings, which did not help him be perky any more. He was acting like a man in love, but his love interest was nowhere to be found. (I, of course, was impervious to this type of vulnerability, but I would have to admit that I had been thinking of Silesia, but nothing worth mentioning, only one to two hours a day.)

After two years, Perky and I could not stand it any longer; together, we approached the editor once more. We would have tried going back on Homo Sap's boat, but the day after our arrival home, Perky and I went back to the spot from which we disembarked and the boat had disappeared. (Why did we go back to the boat? Even then the urge to jump back on and go back was present just a day after we arrived?)

"Probably stolen," Perky tried to rationalize its non-presence.

"Hey, boss!" I said as I entered his office. "Remember those articles on Homo Sap? How about doing another run at him?"

"UFOs," the editor murmured, as if he had not heard me. His black rimmed-glasses never looked up, as he continued to mutter: "I need stories on UFOs."

"No, boss," I averred, probably being honest with my editor for the first time. "Homo Sap never talked about UFOs and I never saw anything extraterrestrial down there."

"UFO stories are really HOT," the editor blurted, looking wildly about the office. Then, he fixed his gaze on me, eyes wide open like a madman. "You can go anywhere, if you tell me you can find a story on UFOs."

"Boss, I know there is a story on UFOs in the heart of nowhere," I changed my tune. "If anyone knows about UFOs, Homo Sap would be the one."

"Great, I'll get you the tickets today," The editor shrieked with glee and laughed. His cackle went through the walls, and one could watch its passing through the news room as everyone looked up one-after-another in a wave, shocked.

"Not on the *SS Sea Galahad*," although startled, myself, I determinedly negotiated.

"No, not on the *SS Sea Galahad*," the editor agreed a little too freely. "Can't! The *SS Sea Galahad* went down with all hands on the high seas, the day after it dropped you off."

"Boy, am I glad to hear that," I stated sarcastically.

"UFOs," the editor started muttering again. "I need some stories on UFOs."

"Boss," I interjected as I left the room. "I think you *need* a vacation."

So, back Perky and I went. The boat was not the SS Sea Galahad, but the SS Sea Lancelot, the SS Sea Galahad's sister ship. When we saw the boat, which looked older and more decrepit than the *SS Sea Galahad*, something I had thought not possible, Perky and I looked at each other and just walked on board. This time we were both DETERMINED. Down to South America we went, bailing out water most of the time. Then we retraced our steps and found the "disappearing river", as the natives used to refer to it. Finally we were back in Homo Sap's camp, and there he was, swinging in his hammock with a sombrero over his head.

"Welcome back, Norman and Perky," Homo Sap spoke to us without lifting the cap.

"Yes," I replied. "We are back."

Perky was jittering and jerking in the background as he saw many of the tribe's people showing up, including his favorite beautiful women. A couple of them arrived with a child in tow. This was this man's heaven, and he wanted to get re-acquainted. He looked like the happiest man in the world.

"Go," Homo Sap raised himself up, taking the sombrero off and pointing toward the assembled throng. "Meet your family, Perky!"

No more needed to be said and Perky shot off. Among the crowd was another beautiful woman, but she was not part of Perky's entourage. Nervously, I tried to ignore her, but I was also pleased to see her again. (God, what is happening to me? Am I, too, going to succumb to going native? Will I renounce my "modern" human stature to become a savage? BUT, she is so beautiful!)

"Ah-humpf," Homo Sap cleared his throat. Obviously, there had been a noticeable pause in the dialogue. ("How long had I been staring at Silesia?" I thought to myself, horrified and embarrassed, that I had let my civilized guard down so completely.)

"Yes, well," When in doubt, ignore the problem; so I launched into an interview with Homo Sap. The economy was not doing well, when I left; so I thought that would be a good place to restart our conversations. "In my world, the country is not doing very well financially."

"That does happen," Homo Sap affirmed, ready to take in my opening statement.

"A huge number of people are being put out of work and they have eaten up all of the government's unemployment reserves and are going to cost us taxes." I was eager to point out to Homo Sap what I'd hypothesized all along.

"All these laws encouraging people to go on workman's compensation or welfare were just ruining the stamina of the individual to look after himself."

Homo shook his head sadly when he heard this comment.

"You people do not grow up very fast, do you? Let me tell you a story about the days before social security and welfare in your land."

"I have come three thousand miles and you're going to recite to me a story from my own world?" I admonished him. "My editor is going to have a fit over this."

"That's where it happened," Homo Sap stated simply. "Do you want to hear it or not?"

"Bird-speak, again," I mumbled and grumbled.

"Yes," Homo Sap smiled.

There was a short silence as I looked around to see if Silesia was still around and oddly I was disappointed to see that she had disappeared. (Although she was curious upon our arrival, she is probably married now, I glumly thought to myself. Now I was doubly embarrassed at my earlier *faux pas!*)

"Go ahead," I succumbed to Homo Sap's twisted sense of humor; I was depressed. Whether this was due to my disappointment about the story Sap was preparing to tell me or about Silesia having left so quickly was hard to say. I did not want to look at the source of my unhappiness.

Homo Sap began with an understanding nod.

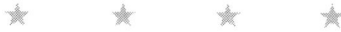

✳   ✳   ✳   ✳

A long time ago, near a great big city, there lived an old woman and her grandson. His mother had died from diphtheria. They lived in an old wooden lean-to shed with a door, but no window in the window opening. The sun kept it fairly warm during the day in winter, but in summer, it was hot and smelled of the pigs that used to live in it. There were always flies in it, even in winter.

Times were hard, but they grew harder. Hungry men roamed the woods and streets looking for jobs and food. It was harder and harder for the grandmother to find work or food as she went from door to door of rich people's houses begging for work in return for food. While the little boy could walk, he went with his grandmother, helping to look for food scraps in garbage bins or kitchen middens. But one summer he came down with polio. He was so badly crippled that he could only lie on the couch and watch the buzzing flies as they flew in and out of the shed through the open-framed window, while his grandmother worked or hunted for food. He was very lonely.

"You are not alone. God is with you." His Grandmother said.

When she found food, the Grandmother fed the boy first. If there was not enough for two, she fed her beloved grandson what she had and went hungry that night.

Cold weather came. The little boy shivered, and the grandmother piled over him all the rags and newspapers she could find to keep him warm. She knelt on the floor besides the couch and hugged him to share with him as much of her body warmth as she could. When he fell asleep, she would curl up in a tattered, broken down armchair and wait for the first light so that she could go hunting for work or food again.

Each day it grew harder to find food in the rubbish bins, and rich people would not allow a tattered, grubby old beggar to work in their house.

"She might have a disease," the relatively wealthy people she asked for help shuddered, as they shut their doors in her face. Now there were days when both the boy and the grandmother had nothing to eat. The little boy cried because he was so cold and hungry, but his grandmother hugged him and said, "Tomorrow will be better."

One night the grandmother died of cold and hunger.

When day came, the little boy called out, "Grandmother, I need you. I want to use the chamber pot. Help me." His grandmother did not answer.

"I am hungry, grandma, please wake up," the little boy cried over and over, but his grandmother would never again wake up—not in this world at least.

After a few days, the little boy was too weak from hunger and cold to call out anymore. He whispered, "Are you here, God?"

Then he, too, died.

A January thaw hatched out more flies. They buzzed loudly every-time they flew drowsily in and out of the sunshine coming through the window opening. They were well fed and content within the shelter of the shed.

"After awhile, some people said, "Haven't seen the old lady around lately. Musta moved away to find better pickin's. Sure enough ain't much to pick at here."

Someone said, "Maybe they's dead. Let's call the police."

Two policemen came. One of them shooed the flies away from the door and went inside. In a minute one came back out, holding his nose, and said, "There are two bodies inside. No signs of violence. Seem to have died from starvation and cold, the grandmother first and then the boy. Better get help to remove the cadavers."

A crowd had gathered, and one young girl cried out, "Don't call them cadavers! Those dead bodies are the empty temples of two suffering souls!"

"A tall, hungry looking man grunted, "Where was God? Why did He let this happen?"

The weeping girl's father, his arm comfortingly around her heaving shoulders, retorted, "Don't ask where God was, Man! Where were WE that we allowed such a thing to happen? God promised us Free Will, and He doesn't break His promises. Our Will, not His, prevailed here."

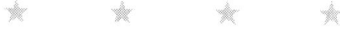

* * * *

Homo Sap paused, while we wiped our eyes and blew away our sniffles.

"Here was a woman who tried to work non-stop until it killed her, supporting a dependent child. She tried desperately to take care of herself and the child, but you're right, she did not have the stamina. Is this what you meant?"

"Yes, no," I answered, confused as to what I really meant.

"A year or two later, Social Security and Welfare were created and helped to cushion people through the economic downturns between WWII and now." Homo Sap continued. "But I look around your world today and note in Congress, members who have never been out in the streets where these things still happen. If they had, there would be no budget impasse. They would have put the children, the poor and the needy first."

"But Defense comes first," I defended my Congress. (What a silly thing to do, I realized afterwards.)

"What is more important, defense or the people you are trying to defend?" Homo Sap asked.

I did not have an answer.

"It is small consolation that God will surely treat Grandma and her grandson to the best of everything in Heaven, while those people in the governments of any nation of the world, who were not there to answer the needs of their electorate, may suffer for what they did not do. It is gratifying to the vengeful to consider that God might even send them back to suffer a fate similar to that of Grandma and her grandson." He paused and cleared his throat. "I am a merciful man; I hope they change their minds before they destroy themselves."

"Destroy themselves?" I sparked up. "What do you mean?"

"Don't you have an adage about even the worm turning on its oppressors? Push the people far enough and they may rebel, destroying their country and their oppressors in the bargain."

On Irony

"I've got to leave," Perky announced to both Homo Sap and I. The tone of desperation was evident in the sound of his voice. We were both in the clearing near Homo Sap's hammock, discussing the local geography.

"We just got here," I responded, a little frustrated with the young man before me.

"I know, I know," Perky wrung his hands like Lady Macbeth.

"Why, I thought you loved it here, Perky," I replied, remembering all the nights he spent dancing with the tribe's women.

"I want to get back to Sylvia and Rebecca and Susie!" He moaned.

"But when you were with them, you couldn't wait to get away from those three!" I cried in desperation. Sometimes Perky's easy ability to make relationships with the opposite sex made me irritated with him, possibly out of envy. I was still somewhat Victorian, looking for that perfect female, who had to look like that perfect female. The problem was I didn't know what that perfect female looked like (even if she paraded herself in front of me everyday), or I didn't want to admit I did know.

"This is different," Perky declared. "Then, I wanted to get here; now I want to get away from here."

"That is somewhat ironical," Homo Sap smiled wisely (Can a Homo sap be wise? Somehow I thought that to be an oxymoron.).

"NO," Perky screamed and then whimpered: "This is disturbing. All I want to do is be with Biaka. No other woman interests me anymore. She has bewitched me. Women are insidious."

"The *Bible* says that Jesus was the Fisher of men," Homo Sap ignored Perky's distress, although he was pacing back and forth across the clearing

66

like a caged tiger. "In truth, women are the real fishers of men. They sit on the side of the cosmic pool, stars gleaming off the black surface, and throw in their hooks and wait patiently. Sometimes they hook what they want and sometimes not."

"Are you saying I am a fish?" Perky stopped pacing and glared at Homo Sap?

"Are you not struggling like a fish on a hook?" Homo Sap ignored the baleful look from Perky. "Are you not trying to throw that hook outside of your mouth and move on to the next tempting chunk, which you are imagining is waiting for you on another hook?"

"I'll never eat fish again," Perky declared.

"Yes you will," the Noble Savage laughed. "The problem is not the fish, but the fact that the fish can no longer imagine a better hook."

"I just want to go home," Perky felt he did not need any further explanations; especially one's that irritated the heck out of him. He grasped for the most convenient excuse and hung on for dear life. "That's it! I'm homesick."

"Don't you just want to escape Biaka?"

"Yes, no," Perky looked like a cornered peccary.

"Irony is a wonderful thing," Homo Sap stated, appearing to change the subject. "You want to be with Biaka all the time, but you are also scared to death to be with her."

"Don't taunt me," Perky cried.

"Irony is cosmic humor." Homo Sap went to his hammock and lay down. "This is how I know God has a sense of humor, He gave us irony."

"This is not funny," Perky stated with a very dour face.

"Not to you, now," Homo Sap admitted. "Your mind and life experiences are not broad enough for you to enjoy this type of humor, but one day hopefully they will be and you may even smile at yourself–then."

"Impossible," Perky declared.

"The only time something is impossible is when you are dead." Homo Sap disagreed. "Of course, impractical is another matter."

"Can we leave?" Perky queried like a pleading child. "Please, please?"

"I don't know," I told him forlornly. I was a little depressed and did not want to admit it, so this decision was hard for me. "I think we should stay. At least, let's think about it for a few days."

"Now, this is doubly ironical," Homo Sap started to laugh. "The person, who wants to stay, wants to leave, and the one who wants to leave wants to stay!"

Both Perky and I stared at Homo Sap as if he was a madman, and maybe the irony of this situation is that he is mad, but in the end, he was right.

Computers and the Universe

"I love computers!" I told Homo Sap as I rocked in one of his hammocks, listening to the soughing of the wind in the boughs of the giant trees from which they were strung. "I have five, each more powerful than the rest. I've moved from floppy disks to hard disks, from PCs to main frames–well, almost. I haven't got a mainframe yet, but I can dream, can't I?"

"Of course, the computer isn't a new invention," Homo Sap observed.

"I know that!" I replied crossly. "An Englishman, Charles Babbage, invented the first computer about the middle of the 19th century (1833). Oliver Wendell Holmes mentions it in his *Autocrat of the Breakfast Table*."

"Oh, there were computers around before Babbage. I had one of the best–my own brain," Homo Sap stated with unusual modesty, and chuckled as he tapped his forehead. "Top of the line mainframe, you might say."

He agreed that computers can do almost anything MAN wants them to do, and that, he said, is the key to their power. The computer is built on Aristotelian yes-no logic, so it can give back only what the user puts in. The question is the answer. When we put in our computations about a probable answer, the answer we get is based on the implied question we've asked. The computer has no world outside our own human logic–and its biases.

I told Homo Sap how impressed I am with the fabulous picture of the universe a few thousand years after the BIG BANG, which the computer describes so graphically from the scientific data, it was given.

Homo Sap laughed. "It may be worth a Nobel Prize–and yet be only a fable. According to the built-in Aristotelian yes-no logic, the computer's answer is only as valid as the question, no matter how valid it may seem."

"After all," Sap continued, "If there were unicorns, and if they were white, it would be true that IF there were unicorns, they **would** be white, wouldn't they?"

"Of course," I muttered, "*if* there **were** unicorns."

(At least computers make honest statements–they aren't deceptive. Besides, there *are* unicorns; that's what a one horned rhinoceros is.)

"Yes, they are naive, but, sadly," Homo Sap added, "our computers can be so easily deceived by what humanity thinks of as reality. My friend and I saw five stumps sticking out of the water. We thought we could cross over the slimy green pool to the other side by stepping first on to one stump, then the other. They looked solid enough. HE trusted his new stellar chip computer with a solar battery, which said they were stumps, but my instincts set me to thinking. What are the stumps growing out of? They might be stumps, but suppose they were really fingers joined to something under the dark water? Suppose that SOMETHING was the hand of a giant ogre waiting to trap me for dinner? I told my friend that I had a hunch the pond was dangerous and said that "Computers are not infallible."

My friend tossed aside this sacrilegious thought with a roll of his eyes and said he trusted his latest model computer implicitly. He attempted to cross the pool in spite of my warnings. There *was* an ogre and he did TRAP something for his dinner–my poor friend...."

Homo Sap sighed heavily and said, "Still, what else can we do except study the pieces until we can figure out the existence of a black HOLE? But we still won't know where the WHOLE came from?"

"Yep! Computers are great, no matter what Sap says! I love them. Even if I asked them to prove we didn't exist," I bragged to Homo Sap, "I'll bet they could prove it, if I asked the right questions to steer it to the answer I wanted."

Homo Sap agreed with my assertion. "I once proved by the law of aerodynamics that bees can't fly–except they do!"

Which just goes to show, I said smugly to myself, that every question we ask the computer has a RIGHT answer, even if it is not true–or even if it is true.

On The Ancient Greeks

Homo Sap and I were having a philosophical discussion about Democracy.

"Very likely," I said, "Democracy was due to a physically oppressive environment, which promoted a romantic perspective of freedom to spring up among the Greeks, not only in their politics, but in their wonderful sculpture, poetry, dramatic works, even their religion."

"I thought they had a wonderfully harmonious relationship with nature?" Homo Sap pondered.

Homo Sap chewed thoughtfully on a *papaw* while he considered the matter. Finally he said, "While it is true that the environment does affect the way man has to live in different climates—he certainly has to wear clothes in the arctic and take them off in the tropics—it is doubtful that it had such an effect on the Grecian pantheology. It was only at a late date in their history that the Ancient Greeks recorded their harmonious relationship with the cosmos."

"You don't think it was a spontaneous outburst of cultural feeling due to the harshness of life?" I asked disappointedly. "Hesiod wrote books on farming that portray a grim picture of man pitted against a truculent earth."

"No, I don't. The whole thing grew out of an aggregation of ancient oral songs and stories. The Greeks, like the Persians, the Hindus, the Latins, the Macedonians [Albanians], Celts and Germans were all part of the same Indo-European racial group, and their view of the cosmology was essentially the same, including their pantheology of nature gods. Every tribe in the world has some sort of sky god. After all, the sky is there, isn't it, with all those strange moving bodies of light? The Indo-Europeans were no different than

70

any other people. The Hindu Dyaus-pitar, Greek Zeus-pitar, Latin *Ju-piter* or **Deus pater** are the same god with the same functions."

"But," I protested, "On such an animistic basis, nature gods with the same functions, but different names, could have sprung up in any culture anywhere!"

Homo Sap shrugged indifferently. "Who knows? As descendants of Paleolithic man, perhaps the Greeks inherited their cosmology from the Magdalenian artists."

"You may be right," I replied eagerly. "After all, the artists in these two cultures, though separated by time and by achievement, seem to have uniquely experienced the beginning and development of a visual perspective technique, creatively responding to the dominant anxiety and tensions of their time."

"That's high faluting talk," Homo Sap replied. "What do you mean?"

I warmed to my subject. "Well, for the prehistoric people, tension related to dealing with an omnipotent environment that contributed to their art, and they painted their way out of this tension with magical symbols on their cave walls. The Greeks endeavored to resolve conflicts stemming from the character of their social organization by the invention of a dimensional democracy."

"Hmm!" Homo Sap almost snorted. "If social organization includes the aggressive tendency of the ancient Hellenes to rape, rob, kill and enslave their neighbors, including their own cousins, the Helots, you may be right."

"You are being a little unfair," I countered. "The Greeks had so many enemies. Could they help it if they were always at war?"

"Well," Homo Sap smiled, "I agree that many people in those times could not choose their fate, but in the main the Greeks were responsible for most of their own problems. The Egyptians, for many centuries, were a relatively peaceful people whom the Greeks raided constantly, much as their Viking cousins raided the seacoasts of Europe and even Asia at a later date. It should have been no surprise to the Hellenes if their neighbors retaliated with equal venom. But the ferocious Greeks carried all before them. Look at Ilium before it was destroyed by Grecian treachery."

"I thought you liked the ancient Greeks, that you respected their wonderful civilization."

"Oh, I did–I do! I honor them particularly for their unbiased honesty about themselves and their actions."

"They were the founders of our Democracy."

"Indeed they were an oasis of rationality," Homo Sap agreed, "in a desert of barbarism. We owe them not only for the concept of Democracy, but the basis of many of our current scientific achievements. Except for the solar battery (and even that may have had its roots in ancient Egypt), hardly any of Western Man's scientific ideas are exactly new hat."

"Well?" I asked crossly, "Why do you talk as if the Greeks were some kind of savages?"

"Weren't they?" Homo Sap asked amusedly. "Do you think that Odysseus' act in seizing Hector's little son out of his mother's arms and braining him on a rock was that of a civilized man? Politically expedient, perhaps–no son of Hector would grow up to challenge the Greeks–but...civilized?"

"O-O-Odysseus was a hero!" I stammered.

"Not in the eyes of Andromache, Hector's enslaved widow. From her point of view, Odysseus was a merciless baby-killer. Whether a person is a saint or a demon is all in the point of view–or that of the storyteller," Homo Sap responded lazily. "What is surprising was that some of those Greek savages grew up enough to envision a democracy, at least for those who were landed, rich, educated and native born. Foreign-born people could not become citizens, although their Grecian born children might. Nor did Greek democracy extend to the slaves or the common man. Woman, of course, was not included, either."

"But–but–all men and women are equal in the sight of God," I stammered.

"The idea that all men and women are equal in the sight of heaven" he shrugged dismissively, "was not propounded until much later by a Jewish carpenter named Jesus of Nazareth, who had got the notion from the Egyptians. And it took more than a thousand years for this revolutionary notion to penetrate into Western law. Even now it is hotly contested in many parts of the world."

"Not in the USA," I responded happily. "Our Revolution took care of that–you know–freedom and liberty for all!"

Homo Sap cleared his throat apologetically. "As a matter of fact, not only were slaves and women **excluded** from suffrage by the Founding Fathers, but the early American patriots did not even include the lower class white man in their new democracy. Landless men and men of low income were also excluded. They had to wait for Andrew Jackson, in 1828, to offer general suffrage—for white men only. Personally, I think that, although there were many other causes, the seeds of the Civil War began at this time; If white

MEN had the vote, why not **BLACK** men, too? Although black men got the vote in 1865 in theory, American *women* of *any* color did **NOT**."

I tried to get my own back. "You see, in the end, women *were* affected by the environment–the environment of freedom."

Homo Sap grinned. "Sexy wives have powerful means to affect their masculine environment," he agreed, "as the Greek Aristophanes noted in his comedy, *Lysystrata*. The far more likely truth is that men feared that, if freed, their sisters, wives and daughters could do a better job of running their own lives than the men had been doing—a life that might not necessarily include them. Maybe American men had an epiphany; they looked around at the mess their own sex had made, and hoped their women could do a better job. Remember it was an **ALL MALE ELECTORATE** that voted for Women's Suffrage in 1922."

Fire!

"This is all your fault," I yelled at Homo Sap, shaking my newspaper in his face. "Look at this!"

"What's my fault?" Homo Sap asked, taking the paper out of my hand and running his eyes over the headlines by the light of the campfire. "New Cure For Wrinkles? I told them years ago to use lard...Incumbents voted in...Oh, Female recruits in army sexually abused. I'm not in the army...I'm no lecher."

"Well, you Okayed the idea of women in the army. You know how it is. Put a lighted match near a piece of paper, and you're going to have a fire."

"Women are lighted matches? They set men on fire?"

"You know what I mean! If you put men and women together, they'll have sex."

"No, I don't know anything of the kind. Put *animals* together and you may have indiscriminate matings, but human beings who have been taught to value themselves and the opposite sex refrain from animalistic behavior."

"Everyone knows that sex is the strongest pull in life," I grumped. "That's why farmers separate young roosters from the pullets; why heifers are kept from the bull until the females have reached full maturity; why boys and girls had separate schools in olden days, to protect them from each other until they had reached years of reasoning."

"I agree that vulnerable adolescents need protection from their own instincts until they have reached maturity. All male or all female schools for a year or two in their teens may allow them time to come to terms with their sexual instincts while developing full awareness of the potentials of their own gender. In the end, they must intermingle with each other. The lighted

74

match must avoid the tempting paper; the vulnerable paper must not come too close to the match. It's a matter of training, of self-respect."

"You mean you still think men and women should battle together?" I was appalled. The jungle seemed closer; the shadows darker behind the rosy curtain of flame that danced over the logs of the fire.

"Together, but not with each other."

"But think of the sparks and raging blazes!"

"We are talking about men and women, not match sticks and paper. Men and women should have learned to be accountable for their own behavior by the time they were drafted for military duty."

"But those women flung themselves at their instructors? Where was their moral training?"

"Sounds like a lame excuse to me! Adam passing the buck as usual! If true, where was the training, moral or military, of the men and women who became these human matches?" Homo Sap asked dryly, as he leaned forward and put another stick on the campfire to warm up the area about it. Although fires are mostly for light, even in the jungle, the temperature drops a little at night and a fire is comforting. It keeps away the noxious night insects as well as predatory animals. "Shouldn't trained warriors (male and female) be so self-disciplined they can say no to temptation?"

He cogitated a moment while I warmed my hands, chilled more from shock than cold.

"Reminds me of the teacher who stole three times before she was arrested. Either she had kleptomania and couldn't help herself, or she was a punishment freak and wanted to be arrested. Maybe this abuse of authority is signaling that these army instructors are sick and want to be thrown out of the army."

"The army isn't filled with nuns and monks," I fired back.

"Of course not," Homo Sap looked at me in surprise. "It's presumably filled with rational human beings, disciplined to control their urges for the honor of the service. If they lack that discipline, they don't belong in the army, certainly not in positions of authority."

He cleared his throat.

"Actually, they don't belong among Homo sapiens either…maybe some subhuman branch. But that may be unfair to lesser animals. After all, they can't help being what they are. With our mental computers," he pointed proudly to his head, "*we* can."

"Although I am not married or have children, I do have a niece, named Eva. No daughter or niece of mine is going into the Army, no matter what you say," I yelled, and a flock of monkeys and parakeets were startled into full flight from the surrounding trees. I ducked to avoid their onslaught of falling dung. "You know what an army on the rampage is like. Theirs, or ours, demoralized by the heat of battle, are a gang of killers and rapists. Think of My Lai, Maymudiya, Haditha!"

"Think of society in general. Your daughter, if you ever have one, or niece will be like other men's daughters in the Army of Life," Homo Sap replied quietly. "Every day women face these slurs and slanders, the hoots, the cat-calls, the bottom pinching, the breast touchers and thigh feelers, the suggestive sexual innuendoes. Even in peacetime, even in civilian life, they face the same fates as in war: rape, torture and death."

"Well," I replied defensively, thinking uneasily about that lonely walk to her dorm that my niece takes across the campus after classes–I must tell her never to walk alone! "What do you suggest as a cure?"

"If such behavior is a sickness, it ought to be anticipated and controlled. If there is a dereliction of duty, punishment and retraining are vital." He thought a moment and added, "If religious training won't work, good manners might," Homo Sap responded. "But you have to start early in childhood. In many cases of so-called harassment, I don't think the parties involved knew how to court each other. Dancing classes from kindergarten on would be a good start, the minuet, for example."

"Courting classes?" I hooted. "Dancing classes? Now you are joking."

"Mating rituals work for most animals," he responded quietly. "So does training. Starting early enough with the calf, we can train elephants large enough to crush us with their foot to be gentle and obedient. Perhaps we ought to let nature, trained to the habit of self-restraint help us. If, as you say, the sexes are lighted matches and helpless paper, let's train them to know how to safely approach each other without starting a bonfire. Where better than in a dancing class where the touching and feeling are regulated by the rules of the dance? Where the boy steps up and asks formally for the dance. Where, when a girl formally and most politely refuses him, he may learn to control his instincts and take his refusal like a gentleman and an officer, not a bully, nor a sadist taking advantage of his authority, a rapist."

The Stand Off

In the Middle Ages, love was regarded as a violent disease, disastrous to those it attacked. While the victims could be any age, those most likely to be inflicted by this illness were teenagers suffering from the usual adolescent hormone imbalance, since their sanity was not yet fully stabilized. These love-struck youths tended to run in gangs and terrorize their more conservative neighbors. They wore strange hairstyles, painted their faces, sang strange songs and used strange verbal signals to communicate with each other. As far back into the days of ancient Rome and Greece, back into the prehistoric days of Homo sap, adolescents, fallen sick from love, starved themselves, killed themselves or their rivals, or committed suicide for the object of their affections. They ran away, eloped, followed each other across their world, created bastard offspring and generally behaved like modern teenagers. I knew this, but found it difficult to comprehend that essentially nothing had changed except our weapons, transportation and sanitation.

"People haven't advanced far from savagery over the last few thousand years," I told Homo Sap bitterly. "Man is still an ape in fancy dress."

Homo Sap looked at me sympathetically. "What happened to your Rousseau's Noble Savage concept?"

"My niece, my sister's daughter, was held at gunpoint by a suicidal, murderous maniac," I replied. "No," I answered the unspoken question in his compassionate eyes. "She escaped unharmed. The young man is in jail, awaiting trial."

"I had not heard about this," Homo Sap said gently. "Lean back against the palm tree and tell me about it. Perhaps it will help you to talk to a friend."

Dropping my head on my chest, I stretched out my legs on the mossy ground and complied. "My sister brought the boy into her house. He'd had a bad deal and she thought she could help him. She should have known better. His sickness nearly destroyed my niece."

"Kindness is never lost," my host murmured gently as the palm fronds rippled above us. "Was the youth always so vicious?"

"His parents were divorced. Each remarried other mates. The boy had difficulties with the new arrangements and, after doing some acting out, ended up in a foster home. At 18, he was told he had to leave within a week. Someone else was taking his place. ("I thought the foster family liked me," he told my niece as he held her at gunpoint.) No home, no job, no diploma, he was out on the streets, living hand to mouth, sleeping over at this friend's house one night, or at another friends' the next. He was only a desperate boy without means of support."

"If he was so desperate, how did your niece escape?"

"She kept her head—kept him talking. He said he loved her and meant to kill her, then himself. He had sawed the barrel off a shotgun, the handle as well, so that it wouldn't be conspicuous under his coat."

"He hated your niece so much?"

"No, he loved her too much and couldn't take her rejection. He assured her he was going to shoot her in the chest. She was too beautiful to have her face ruined with a bullet. The last thing he wanted to see was her lovely face when he pulled the trigger and shot himself in the head."

"The boy was ill. Surely there is some agency to take care of the mentally disturbed? Surely, there was someone..."

"A juvenile at 17," I replied with bitter emphasis, "he could be helped. The minute he turned 18, he was an *adult*."

"No one was responsible for him?" Homo Sap seemed appalled. "What about his tribe? His kinfolk?"

I shrugged my shoulders dismissively. "His father may have welcomed him for Sunday dinner, even if his new wife didn't. Not every Sunday, of course. Or the boy may have had too much pride to drag himself pathetically to his father's door and beg for assistance."

"You are sad for him?"

"Yes," I replied angrily. "I know that what he tried to do to my niece was a terrible thing, but he is still the same desperate, sensitive child today that he was yesterday."

"What is going to happen to him?"

"The courts will probably put him in jail for a few years or so."

"What?" Homo Sap was shocked. "No one will care for him, mend his spirit, and show him the path to health and happiness? In two or three years, with props to hold the trunk straight, the young palm will grow strong and sturdy and fruitful."

"This palm will be among other sickly, crooked palms and his stem will be permanently bent out of shape," I replied sardonically. "Jails appear to be training grounds for future evil doing."

"Such training in wrongdoing is very costly to the community," Homo Sap remarked seriously. "Would it not be less expensive, less dangerous to the community, to heal the sickness in his soul?"

"Until he kills someone," I replied, "nobody will bother with his problems, and my sister can't mend him. No one will bother with my problems, either. To keep my niece safe, after he comes out, my sister may have to take her family, leave her home, her friends and start over elsewhere—never ever sure that this desperate, twisted young male won't seek them out to kill them both in their sleep."

"The irony is that your niece saved not only her life, but the young man's life too." Homo Sap twisted my perspective around, as usual. "I wonder if he realizes that?"

The Lion and the Lamb

Yelling, I rushed into Homo Sap's palm thatched primitive dwelling.

"Sap! Sap!" I shuddered to think that my niece could have been in that very school when those juveniles started shooting. She wouldn't have known what to do—how to save herself. The thought never occurred to me to tell her that, when people start blasting away with guns in an open area, the best thing to do is to drop flat on the ground, arms folded over your head, while you begin to inch away from the site on your belly like a worm. What a helluva thing it is that parents should have to give combat lessons to their kids!

"What's the world coming to? WHAT ARE PEOPLE THINKING," I ended up shouting at the top of my lungs to the astounded Sap, "when little kids start mowing each other down at school with guns?"

"Their senses, I hope," Homo Sap replied, motioning for me to sit down on a straw mat.

"What do you mean?" I was aghast at his off-hand demeanor.

"Until Man realizes what a dangerous wild animal he is, and accepts that he must tame himself and his children, humanity is doomed to live in a jungle." The Noble Savage replied calmly.

I was dazed. "We don't live in a jungle. You do." I looked around in disgust at his primitive huts with the firestones in the center of the clearing. Steam from the stew in the baked clay *olla* cradled within the embers was curling up towards the fire-hole in the roof. "We have skyscrapers and plumbing and computer web sites. We have chairs and couches and real kitchens—with electric stoves."

"Jungles are places where voracious wild animals, human or otherwise, live out their primal urges, fighting, killing, mating, without regard to the feelings or rights of others, knowing no law except that of tooth and claw."

"What do you mean?" I snarled. "We live in a civilized world with rules, goddammit!"

"What use are the rules, if the people are too unprincipled to obey them?" Homo Sap passed me a coconut shell cup filled with *tetli-tetli*, a soothing, and fragrant native brew. "From what you tell me, many humans seem like tigers, stalking the unwary. Buildings, clothes and money don't make a civilization. Even bees build hives and have an orderly social structure. But can we call them civilized? You live in a world which loves violence, which clubs baby seals, considers fishing and hunting a sport, puts guns into the hands of its children. Even your so-called justice is violent. People scream hang him, or shooting isn't good enough for her. You have great cities, which soar to the skies, but they are filled with angry people some of whom say to each other—where children can hear them: 'I'd like to strangle them with my bare hands for their outlandish views on color or country.' Is it any wonder that your children are violent, too? Hitler had handsome cities and trains and planes. Was he civilized?"

I grudgingly admitted that Hitler was not a good model for urbanity. Neither was the African premier who, while building a cathedral so large that aeroplanes could fly through its nave, neglected the rights of human beings for whom he was responsible.

"Humanity," Homo Sap pontificated, "will never make much progress in civilization until it concedes that Man is a treacherous, vicious animal. Although every child born is a *tabula rasa*, on which new and better things can be written, if those new and better things are not written, it may also become—or have the potential to become—a ferocious, cunning, cruel and dangerous beast."

"How can you say that?" I protested, "My little niece was the cutest little kitten of a child—"

"True, but no more true than the fact that tiger cubs and even wolf cubs are charming in their babyhood, showing no enmity to any species. Didn't Julian Huxley found a children's zoo in London to prove the point? That all young animals, including children of all races and creeds, even though as different in kind as the carnivorous lion cub and the herbivorous lamb, could learn to live together peacefully and happily?"

Homo Sap had lost me. I thought frantically. Who was Julian Huxley? Oh, yes, one of Tom Huxley's sons. I'm not into that kind of nature study; I'm better acquainted with the works of Julian's brother Aldous, the famous writer. Puzzled, I asked, "What's Huxley's zoo got to do with the problem of children killing children?"

"A lot, really," he replied dryly. "For even animals ape their elders. If a child sees violence in the streets, in the home, on the TV, like the tiger cub, that child will equate adulthood with violence. Without proper gentling and feeding, children or tiger cubs grow up to be lethal predators. If hungry or frightened they more easily revert to their feral instincts."

I was affronted. "Are you insinuating that my little niece will grow up to be a wild animal?"

"Not if you, or your sister, give her the knowledge she needs."

I brightened up. "My sister's town has a great school system, lots of advanced science courses, computer education, physics," I reported. "They even have a band, a winning football team, a drama society and a gun club."

Homo Sap looked at me sadly. "You don't understand, do you? Like Hitler, Henry VIII, Oliver Cromwell, Ivan the Terrible and Stalin were all well educated. Even the serial killer, Ted Bundy, was highly literate. But no one bothered to tame them, so they grew up to be sadistic killers."

"We tell our children that killing is a bad thing," I protested. "We punish them for hurting each other."

"Why not prevent them from killing each other by making sure that no child has access to a gun or other lethal weapon—that no household contains lethal weapons a child might use by accident or intent. More people die from gun accidents each year than they do from criminal gunfire. After all, if we won't allow the use, or build up, of lethal weapons in Iraq, why should we allow their use or build up in this country?"

"But suppose someone needs a gun, because he fears someone is out to kill him?

Homo Sap shrugged. "Tell the multi-billionaires of your world to cough up enough money for every town and city to hire so many police that guns would be unnecessary. Any timid soul could ask for 24-hour protection until the aggressor is taken into custody. (The existence of billionaires is obscene in the presence of the poverty, hunger, ignorance and crime, with so much wealth in the hands of so few postulates. Obviously, the more money at the top, the less at the bottom.) Lions and lambs in the zoo are more easily taught than their wild cousins, because they are not hungry or afraid. Feed the children first, and then they will be more likely to accept that humans need not be predators."

"We do," I replied smugly. "We've got laws, telling everybody that they must not commit violent crimes, or they will receive a violent punishment. We've got guards at the street crossings to watch out for children."

Homo Sap shrugged. "The trouble with retaliatory violence is that it creates more violence. Those laws and those guards didn't prevent those children in Colorado or Arkansas from being shot in the schoolyard by other children, did they? Your educational approach is all wrong."

"What do you mean?"

Homo Sap shook his head. "Knowledge of many kinds is taught in your schools, but the fundamental lessons of ethics, principles and manners, the moral training which teaches the individual how to put the brakes on his tendency to violence, is not. It's not enough to point out the difference between a good and a bad action. The desire to avoid evil and the self-control to restrain one's self from violent action must also be taught. Your public schools don't even teach the basic lessons of courtesy and etiquette, which would show vulnerable young people of different sexes the proper way to approach each other, which gives them pride in their own self control. Your world needs universal rituals, a universal code of honor, the same from the east coast to the west coast, for the rich and the poor, on how children and adolescents should approach each other in order to prevent tension filled, potentially violent situations. Today's children, like Adam and Eve in the Garden of Eden, have mental bellies that need to be filled to the brim with apples of knowledge; they lack the moral training to handle life rationally. They can only understand it as it applies to their primitive, passionate, irrational and uncontrolled emotion. So an outbreak of violence is not surprising when the lions and the lambs in your society have not learned to love and live with each other. To have knowledge and no principles is to be capable of unlimited evil. Any amoral child might use the knowledge he has gained to shoot or stab or poison someone."

I was scandalized. "We aren't allowed to teach morals or formal etiquette in the public schools. Etiquette, like dancing, is considered to be an expensive educational frill. Teaching morals borders on the religious and in a public school this is a not allowed."

"Why? Parents need the back-up of their religion or culture to strengthen their attempts to control or civilize the wild beast in their offspring." Homo Sap was startled.

"Why?" I replied smugly, having the answer for once during our conversations. "It's against the law. Morality is considered to be a variable religious subject. It's unconstitutional to mix the tenets of church and state."

Homo Sap was confounded. "Strange," he murmured, "Ethics is the universal core of civilization, isn't it? If so, I would have thought it would be the first subject a modern society would teach, not the last."

Forever Young

Homo Sap was excited. He was actually pacing rapidly, not sauntering, up and down the jungle aisles.

"I have never believed in age," he said, "and now science has proved me right. All mankind should, like the one-hoss shay, live a hundred years or more to the day before crumbling into the dust."

"What brought this up?" I asked, more because he expected an answer than because I was really interested.

"Didn't I just tell you that science—a scientist," he corrected himself, "has located the human turn on, shut off youth cell valve? This means that soon we will be able to prevent the *soma* from falling into the decrepitude caused by dying or defective cells."

I yawned. This scientific mumbo jumbo was beyond me, but he would never let me tell him about winning the football pool before he had talked himself out, so I mumbled, "Yeah? Interesting."

Exasperated, he frowned at me. "Don't you see? This discovery proves my theory. Age, senility, does not exist, only illness. The symptoms we call age, which attack the *soma* or body can be abolished. All of us are dying far too young. Senility is a disease, which robs us of at least half our life. Perhaps more"

I got it. *Soma* meant body. Symptoms meant things like arthritis or wrinkling or withering of the muscles. I rubbed my aching hip; I had a touch of arthritis. It's been bothering me a lot lately, slowing me down. Sure, I was interested. Who wants wrinkles, withered muscles, osteoporosis and slack memory?

"Do you mean we'll stay young forever?" I asked, doubtfully.

"The scientists say our organism is designed to last for six times its maturity. Maturity for man is approximately twenty-five years."

I rubbed my aching hip and did a little figuring. One hundred and fifty years of youth? Wow!

"Will they take volunteer test subjects?" I asked. "Where do I go to volunteer? Gee, I might even get to live forever!"

Homo Sap grinned. "Considering the longevity of the primordial slime from which all living creatures have sprung, that could be a possibility. We should live *as if* we had forever. As a skeptic, I also ask myself how we can tell that all men are mortal, until the last man dies. So I repeat, live as if you are going to live forever. With the help of this youth serum, perhaps you will."

On Sex and Marriage[5]

I was really irked by all the talk about same sex marriages when I set off for the jungle where Homo Sap lives.

Almost the first thing I said to him after accepting a cup of fermented wild grape juice was, "Do you have problems with this same sex marriage bit?"

Homo Sap seemed surprised.

"How do you mean trouble?" He asked.

"Well, you know, homosexuals and lesbians want the right to marry like the rest of us straight people."

He laughed. "We don't have marriages. They aren't necessary. If any pair, male or female, wants to handfast themselves for a year or two or for life, that's their business. Since all property is equally shared, we don't collect property or income taxes. A civil service to prove ownership of property or money by marriage or descent, is unnecessary,"

I was shocked. "No marriage licenses?"

"No marriage licenses, no birth certificates, no death certificates."

"Why not?"

"Well, you see, we don't have a government to support. The shamans keep track of the births so everyone knows who is a sibling or a cousin or a son or daughter."

I was shocked. "Who pays for the kids' support or schooling?"

"We all do. Children are the future of our tribe. To us, every child is precious, because there are so few of us. I know this is not the case outside our untouched jungle. At one time, in the Aleutian Islands off Alaska, it was so hard to feed the tribe that drastic actions had to be taken, when their <u>population rose a</u>bove a certain number. One person too many could cause the

5   August 6, 2004

starvation or death of many. So, when their population limit was reached, if a baby was born, it could only be allowed to live if an older person would die in its stead; otherwise the baby was smothered at birth. The child's death was a sacrifice for the good of the many. Of course, if an infant was thrown to the carnivores, abandoned or murdered simply because it was unwanted, that was an evil of human, not divine, plan, because no good ensued from it."

I shuddered.

"After they left Eden, many of Adam and Eve's descendants forgot the purpose of sex. They didn't know that the combination produced offspring. They thought the gods of Nature induced conception, so they used matrilineality to keep track of relationships. They used the mother's name, because, in a free sexual society, it was easier to determine who their mother was, then, even after they re-discovered the purpose of masculinity, the identity of the male parent."

"Like the Amerinds," I mumbled. "The chief's nephew, his sister's son, was his heir, not his own son."

"Exactly," Homo Sap agreed. "No DNA testing existed then... A wedding ring and a license are not necessary for procreation at all. As for homosexual or lesbian relationships, they are common to most species of birds and animals, which live in groups like Man, seals, cows, cats, dogs or birds. Where females are in short supply, they have multiple husbands. Where the males are in short supply, they have multiple wives. Where sexes are even, the man or woman who takes extra partners is a selfish show-off."

"Why do we have marriage at all?" I growled angrily.

Homo Sap laughed. "That's an easy question to answer. Heterosexual or homosexual, people like to *own* the partners they take. They don't like to share. Heterosexual men jealously want to own a wife or wives for their own pleasure—whether it pleases the women or not. Often enough it doesn't please them, so they play around with other men. That's why harem owners castrated the harem guards, turning them into unsexed eunuchs. Besides, when men piled up wealth, they wanted their own children to inherit it, and not those of another man. Also, when times were hard, they resented having to feed the children of other men, especially if they were having trouble feeding their own."

"So legal marriage was invented to prevent indiscriminate matings producing bastard offspring?"

"Basically, yes, although, like the Eskimos, tribal survival played a part. The early Scandinavians were tough about it. If a boy and girl were caught in the act, they drowned them both in the bogs. But that is not the only reason. Big government requires big taxes to survive. That's why William the Conqueror sent his IRS men all over England, creating the *Doomsday Book*, recording the names of every man born, married or buried in order to make sure that every living Englishman paid his share of the government bill."

"Sir Robert Cooke did that in Massachusetts for the London Company, which established the Pilgrims at Plymouth," I remarked loftily, just to let Homo Sap know he wasn't the only one who knew anything. I added importantly, "But they wouldn't allow single males to live alone. They were more afraid of onanism than homosexuality."

"Masturbation?" Homo Sap smiled. "Why so they were."

"But what has record keeping got to do with homosexual or lesbian marriages?"

"The law has never regarded them as necessary, because they were unproductive for tax purposes or future military enrollments."

"But what about adoption or artificial insemination?"

"What about it? Surely any decent person or persons may adopt and bring up one or more children? Marriage is not necessary for that; money is. As for artificial conception, such births are already enrolled in the hospital and state records for future tax purposes or military service. No marriage is needed to prove line of descent, since the semen or ova donors are often anonymous. I think it is very wrong that a child should not be aware of both sides of his or her birth-line, but at least such a child knows it is wanted, whereas many unfortunate children are brought into the world unloved and unwanted. Marriage is not necessary for an artificial choice by any woman—or, for that matter, man."

"But what about the church? Sodomy and lesbianism are sins—"

"That depends on the point of view of each religion. It has nothing to do with legal marriages, anymore than any other kind of non-productive sexual relationship. Legalizing any conjugal relationship has its hazards for the couple, for, unlike our handfasts, such pairings make them subject to your complicated division of property and assets at death or divorce. Married or single, heterosexuals or homosexuals may will their property to each other, or to any children whom they adopt."

"What about the children? Aren't they better off with a male and female parent?"

"Sometimes, but often, because of deaths and divorce, lone uncles, maiden aunts, grandparents or even older siblings have brought up well-adjusted children. Children of divorce are more at risk, because their parents were ill-adapted or too irresponsible for marriage."

I didn't like to agree with Homo Sap; he is the savage after all. So, I said churlishly. "I suppose you believe that sexual pairings of any kind should be individual agreements, for a day, a year, or a lifetime, but when a child is conceived or adopted, the parents, heterosexual or homosexual, should be condemned to a twenty year marriage."

"Unless every child of that marriage is a cherished and welcome ward of its parents and the state, as they are in our village that would be a reasonable assumption."

The Exquisite Torture

I was walking over to the common *compong* where there was a small cupboard. This *compong* was used for dances during inclement weather, ceremonial meetings and general tribal gatherings. Built solidly with carved wood, the building was reminiscent of a Maori meeting house. The main building was a rectangle of about 40 feet by 25 feet with a small door at the rear that led to a small attached building of 5 by 8 feet that doubled as a staging area for ceremonies and a cupboard for non-staging times. I was looking for an ivory needle to sew together my tattered Western clothing and wondered if this was one of the items that was obtained by the tribe and saved in a small warehouse for communal use.

The time of day was nearing dusk and a greenish glowing twilight filled the main building as I entered. A miasma of flowers and the smells from the nearby jungle mixed to create an enticing, intoxicating perfume. Resolutely, I waded through the light and smells to the small door in the back of the ceremonial house. Opening the door I started through when a vision of beauty froze me in place.

Silesia was standing in the small space with the light of the setting sun streaming through an open window, glistening against her hair, silhouetting in detail the fine lines of her body. Holding a small needle, which she had just plucked from a shelf, she looked over at me and smiled.

"Allo, Norman, 'ow are you?" she stated with a thick accent.

"I—" The cat had definitely got my tongue, but I wish it had taken my whole body. I encountered a state of astonishment that seemed to have stricken my vocal chords. This silence on my part did not appear to bother Silesia at all.

"I 'ave been learning – Engleesh," she stated proudly; she accented the 'Eng' with her pronounced, but fascinating enunciation.

I was like a deer caught in front of headlights and Silesia was the light. She smiled knowing full-well the affect she was having on me. Eschewing the door at the end of the little room, she came forward, and I backed up like an idiot. Unfortunately, the doorway was thin, just two feet wide, and short; so as I backed into the doorjamb, I had to bend forward due to the low lintel and, unwittingly, I only gave Silesia a small space to pass by. Still holding the needle up with one hand, Silesia came up and turned her body to slide through the opening I had left, but she stopped within the doorframe–with me—and looked up—looking deeply into my eyes.

I could smell flowers in her hair and felt her breath upon my face. Only about an inch separated our lips. Her breasts were a gorgeous panoply touching my chest. I could feel them pressing through my thin cotton shirt and one of her legs quietly invaded the space between my legs.

"I need to prac-teese," she said, stressing the 'tice' portion of the word practice. "Maybe you could come by and help me prac-teese? Yes?"

And she waited, smiling, riveting me with her beautiful violet eyes. I was being tortured by the ecstasy of being near her.

"Yes," I burst out finally. Not having taken a normal breath from the moment I had first seen her in the small room, I expelled the word with more force than I expected. With this expulsion of air, I must have inadvertently moved forward as our lips brushed briefly. I began to apologize, but she was already gone. I don't remember her leaving, walking through the main ceremonial building or out the back. She was just gone.

"I must have passed out," I thought to myself. How could she have disappeared so quickly? I was totally upset, but I didn't know if this was due to my inability to respond intelligently or my fear that I was vulnerable to the wiles of a savage. "Have I been infected with that horrible disease called love?"

"I am a civilized man," I declared to myself. "I couldn't be!"

On Understanding Harassment?

Desperate to throw myself into an activity, any activity, after my latest episode with Silesia, I had started a new project. During this short, but intense, period, the Noble Savage sought me out, finding me hidden in a forest clearing about a quarter of a mile from the village. Approximately thirty feet in diameter, the clearing provided a haven from the forest with the light filtering in from above through the various layers of leaves. With the soft green glow from above, I was able to find a measure of calmness, so I could concentrate on the task at hand.

"Yooo," Homo Sap hailed me. "I've been looking for you for quite a while. What are you up to?"

"I am working on a book, and I needed a place that had few distractions." I explained.

"I understand," Homo Sap smiled, all too knowingly. He knew what was distracting me. "So what is the new endeavor about?"

"Remember that harassment thing?"

"Oh, yes," Homo Sap touched his chin thoughtfully. "How did that turn out?"

"I heard through the grapevine that the newspaper settled out of court." I could not admit that bird-speak was the source of my information. "The newspaper did not admit any wrongdoing on my part or their part, but gave the woman a nice settlement to have the issue go away!"

"But I thought you were innocent?" The Noble Savage asked, scratching his head.

"I was," I agreed. "But, the newspaper determined that it was cheaper to offer a settlement than to pay the legal fees."

91

"By not discovering the truth or non-truth, how does your system of justice determine between real, legitimate instances of harassment and these imaginary, money-making schemes?"

"It doesn't," I grumpily admitted. "Appearance is the new truth!"

"So, the civilized don't care what the truth is," the Noble Savage concluded. "Savages, such as myself, can not live without knowing the truth."

"Argh! I don't know anymore!" I admitted agitatedly. "The civilized truth is that I sexually harassed someone, when I didn't. My name has been besmirched!"

"Is there no legal action you can take?" Homo Sap wondered.

"I could take her to court on civil terms, such as defamation of character, but I can not afford the legal fees." I hung my head. "Justice is for the rich; the wealthy are the only ones that can afford it."

"And this experience is leading you to do what?" Homo Sap noted that I was not as rambunctious as normal. Usually, I would be asking the questions.

"I am writing a sexual harassment dictionary to forewarn males of all the various words and phrases that could be considered a form of sexual harassment. For example, I have collated an instance where someone complimented a woman with the phrase that she looked 'absolutely fabulous'. The woman said this made her uncomfortable and the man was soundly reprimanded."

"How can 'absolutely fabulous' be sexual harassment?" Homo Sap quizzically queried. "This just sounds like a compliment to me?"

"It was just a compliment, but because of this reference to the recipient's discomfort I note this to be a new expansion of sexual harassment. Hence, I am adding it to my harassment dictionary."

"So men can no longer compliment women?"

"From this experience, if a woman feels even uncomfortable, regardless whether there is sexual content or not, that is now considered sexual harassment." I concluded.

"I thought civilization is big on free speech? Isn't this free speech?" The Noble Savage curiously questioned.

"Women can determine whether what is said to them is free speech or not, depending upon their feelings." I concluded.

"Doesn't it go both ways?" Homo Sap enquired.

"By law the man has to listen to the woman." I confirmed. "If the woman says 'No', the man has to stop. The implication is that for man to do something, a woman has to say 'Go' at some point. In other words, she is obliged by law to offer platitudes to show her appreciation, while a man cannot."

"You appear to me to be really confused. Is this the normal state of a civilized male?"

"What do you mean by that?" I replied very defensively.

"If women do not allow the men to communicate their interest," Homo Sap pondered, "Civilized men, such as yourself, will get confused and upset, because you do not know what to do to express yourself properly."

"Yeh, I have become a sexual cynic," I sarcastically replied. "I have found so far that 30% of the words in the English language could have a sexual slant and I have just scratched the surface."

"Yes, you look thoroughly confused and a bit overwrought." Homo Sap inquired. "Could it be that you want to – communicate – with someone of the opposite sex and this previous situation is confounding you?"

"I don't want to communicate with anyone!" I screamed. "I just want to work on this damn book!" Obviously, I confirmed Homo Sap's assessment of my emotional state, but I was not going to admit it.

"Well," Homo Sap backtracked. "I guess Jesus Christ was right. The meek shall inherit the Earth."

Puzzled, I merely stared at the Noble Savage.

"Eve was the cause of the downfall of man-kind, leading to the departure from Eden of both kinds, men and women. Due to this one person's single error in judgment, all her kind, all the women of the millennia since have been subjugated. Jesus was well aware of this inequity and when he referred to the meek, who is the meekest of the meek, but women?" Homo Sap clarified. "Now, it is the woman's turn to be in control."

"Egad!" I blurted, as I realized that my own society was systematically and legally emasculating me, but for some reason I could not admit this flaw in my own civilization to this – savage.

"I hope civilization never makes it to the jungle." The Noble Savage continued, recognizing my hesitation. "A tribe like the Tupano would be paralyzed, because their whole cosmos and language is integrated with sexual connotations.[6] Under your type of civilization, the men would never be allowed to speak!"

---

6   Amazonian Cosmos, Gerardo Reichel-Dolmatoff, University of Chicago Press, 1971

Termination Duster: The Sleep Forever Sandman

Homo Sap strolled over as I opened the little silvery packet of snowy dust, the skull and crossbones plainly marked on the front.

"Contemplating sniffing some Termination Dust?" he inquired politely. He hunkered down on the soft moss.

"I have a hangnail. It hurts like hell! The pain is killing me. Why shouldn't I die with dignity?" I snarled defensively.

"Dying is dignified?" Homo Sap's heavy brows went up in mild surprise. "Who says?"

"My cousin's doctor says so, that's who. He's going to help me terminate myself."

"Ah!" Homo Sap nodded wisely. "The DOCTOR has a death wish. HE wants to die, but he's scared to do himself in, probably a religious hang-up."

"What do you mean?"

"The doctor is too chicken to do himself in. He wants a little assistance from the state, execution for murder by electrocution, lethal injection, *etc.*" Homo Sap frowned thoughtfully, "Unless..."

"Unless what?" I demanded.

"Unless your heir is paying him to put you out of the way!"

"Roger?" I was so shocked I forgot the hangnail. "Why should Roger do me in?"

"Don't ask me.

"Now that you mention it, Roger did recommend him."

94

"Some people will do anything for money. Others are like weasels: they kill for the fun of it–their fun–Jack the Ripper types."

"My doctor is not a weasel." At least I hoped not. Then there was my cousin, Roger. Surely he was not waiting for my shoes–actually for my new wheels–that extravagant Jaguar I had treated myself to with some of the proceeds from my syndicated articles? I thought uneasily.

"Of course not," soothed Homo Sap. "He's too smart to kill on the sly. By espousing euthanasia and assisted suicide, though, he can make his kills legally in some places. Think of that!" Homo Sap said dreamily. "Make suicide legal, get yourself a license to kill, then brainwash your victims into asking for an assisted suicide. What more could a serial killer want?"

"My doctor isn't a serial killer. He's helped some of his patients die, but none of their families think the worse of him for that."

"Perhaps that's why the patients let the doctor kill them, because they are broken-hearted–they know their families would be glad to get rid of them." He said meditatively. "Depressed as they were by their lack of loving support, it would have been easy to persuade them to run away from their problems, to die, even if they were not ill, rather than fight for the years of life their God had allotted them."

"Why would people want to commit suicide, if they didn't have something the matter with them?" I asked uneasily.

"Who knows? Hypochondria, perhaps. Mostly loneliness because of the indifference of others to their plight. It is hard to be ill and have to realize that no one wants to come near you because you aren't much fun anymore. If anyone bothered to make them feel wanted or useful in the world, they'd feel no reason to die until the timekeeper at St. Peter's gate shouted: 'Time's up!' Of course, there are people who put away people for profit as well as for pleasure. One woman made a living out of assisted suicides. She would marry a man, get him to put all his money in her name, convince him he had a terminal illness, and then persuade him to commit suicide. She did it quite a few times before she was caught."

"Most people aren't such fools!" I argued.

"No, but many people are very suggestible, especially the very young and the very old, or those who are in great pain. A suicide assistant could rack up record kills that way. More than Ted Bundy in Florida or that fellow Gacy in Chicago… If they had been smarter, they would have become doctors and sanctimoniously arranged their murders to look like suicides–or surgery inexplicably gone wrong."

"I'm not THAT old, and I'm not suggestible, either," I replied, somewhat offended. I was so engrossed in the conversation that my pain had gone away. I stealthily scattered the Termination Dust over some unsuspecting termites and stuffed the empty package in my pant's pocket.

"No, you're just as gullible as the next human to a plausible flim-flam."

"You're practically human yourself," I retorted snidely. "Aren't you gullible, too?"

"Very likely, but I'm woods wary and woods scary. When a carnivorous plant offers me a drink of water, I offer it a fly. I am also wary of individuals who ask for the powers of life and easy death–FOR OTHERS–especially when their assistance is not needed. Even the most helpless need only stop eating to get their wish–if they really want to die. I remind myself that man is a predator. We've been trying to control his instinct to kill every living creature in sight, including his fellow men, for millennia. It's not wise to give certain individuals the power to kill. We all know what power does to men and women. It corrupts, and absolute power corrupts absolutely."

"But a panel of doctors...," I urged weakly.

"That just spreads the power to a board with a Chief Terminator at the head, spreading the dust in everyone's eyes. If health costs are too high, or facilities are filled up, who's to say that the Chief Terminator might decide to terminate anyone on any excuse just to reduce medical costs? For instance, they may withhold treatment for marginal cases. You know, let those harmless cysts grow. If they become malignant, they'll do the killing for you."

"But–but some people are only vegetables," I murmured weakly.

"How do you know? Many, said to be insentient vegetables, are sentient conscious people, listening to those around their unresponsive bodies plotting their murder."

"Look, Sap, you know I'm not talking about THEM. I'm talking about those who live in constant pain, facing an agonizing, certain death."

"Why agonizing? In hospices for the terminally ill, where patients can receive medication on demand, there is no *need* for agony. And ALL of us face the THROES of CERTAIN DEATH, usually unpleasant. I've never met an immortal yet, have you?"

"I'm not immortal, no," I admitted, "and since I want an easy death, it seems to me that assigned terminators might be helpful."

"You trust *MAN* to that extent?" Homo Sap marveled. "I don't. This is a crowded world. From birth, everything on the Earth conspires to do you harm–the heat, the cold, the floods, fires, earthquakes, tornadoes and electrical storms, not to mention viruses, bacteria, molds, prions and other as yet unknown pathogens; carnivorous plants, insects and animals. Even your own species–man–is out to get you."

"That's true," I admitted, thinking it over. "Survival of the fittest, I suppose."

"In a haphazard way," Homo Sap agreed. "It's like you tossing Termination Dust on those healthy, happy little termites. You had no personal grudge against them, did you?"

"What termites?" I asked, and then remembered. "Oh, yes. *Those?* They were just creatures in the grass. I didn't know them personally. How could I have spite against any one of them? I meant them no harm."

"Neither do those insurance companies that find it more convenient to refuse policies to the sick, rather than have to pay for their cure. Healing the slightly ailing healthy is easier than healing the seemingly hopelessly ill–and much more profitable! Yet the science of medicine has grown because of the efforts of past healers like Paracelsus and Hansen who took on the challenge of the incurable. Healers who infused their despairing patients with new hope, urging them to cling to life, not so much for their own sakes as for the countless others who would have better lives because of their concerted efforts to seize days, hours or even minutes out of the jaws of death. Every day, the possibility of a new cure for an old disease is announced. Even for Lou Gehrig's disease there are hopes for alleviation through genetic tailoring–if you are allowed to live long enough to volunteer for the cure."

On Suicide

A few days later, Homo Sap found me despondently thinking about Silesia. She was constantly on my mind. (Am I sick as Homo Sap once related? Is love a mental illness? Was this why I had been contemplating suicide?)

"Hello, Norman," the Noble Savage greeted me at my *keevah*. "Are you still thinking too much and doing too little?"

"Why do you say that," I responded defensively, miserably seated on a wooden bench, pondering a small ant colony.

"Well, you were contemplating Termination Dust a couple of days ago." Homo Sap went right to the heart of the matter. "And your reason really did not sound like the real reason."

"I had a damn hangnail." I retorted sharply. "It hurt like Hell!"

"Does it hurt now?" Homo Sap questioned.

"No," I admitted.

"Usually, when someone considers suicide," Homo Sap continued. "They have what they think is an irresolvable problem. Of course, every problem is resolvable, but when people get into thinking it is irresolvable, they cannot see the solution. Add to that an unbearable pressure and you have the formula for suicide."

When Homo Sap brought up the issue of the unbearable pressure, Silesia and the exquisite torture she was inflicting upon me instantly sprung to mind. I thought to myself: If Silesia is the unbearable pressure, then what is the problem?

"Well, since you are so smart," I blurted out my thoughts sharply. "What do you think my irresolvable problem is?"

98

"You need to decide whether you are a Homo sapiens or a Homo sap!" Homo Sap responded simply. "You envision life as a Homo sapiens as nice, neat, orderly and controlled, while a Homo sap knows that life is messy, damp, wild and as mixed up as one could imagine."

"What?" I was somewhat put back.

"You would recognize the dilemma more, if I put it in the terms you insist on using. Are you going to stay Western, civilized, modern, or go native and become savage?" Homo Sap coughed, trying to hide a chuckle. "Like me!"

"I am a modern man from the great Western civilization; the greatest civilization Earth has ever known."

"And you struggle with that burden every day."

"At least I am not a savage," I spoke with evident disdain, but all those newspaper articles that I read daily in the United States about men and women vainly trying to find answers through violence haunted me, as I questioned whether Western civilization itself qualified as civilized or savage after all.

"What about Silesia?" Homo Sap probed further. "Isn't she at the heart of your dilemma?"

"Absolutely not!" I snapped, blatantly lying.

"You act as if Silesia were a chimpanzee," Homo Sap stated sharply. "She is a woman."

"She is the subject of – ," I said pompously. "My study!"

"Doesn't your analysis realize that you have fallen in love with this woman?" Homo Sap countered. "Ironically, most people in love get sick when they can't be with their loved one. You are making yourself sick trying to stay away from her."

"Nonsense!" I vociferously disagreed. "I have scrutinized you society closely and found no correlation of her emotions and mine."

"You honestly don't realize that you are crazy about Silesia?" Homo Sap quizzed me, ignoring the multi-syllable fluff.

My startled, speechless response spoke volumes about my state of denial. Men who are caught in the grip of a woman's glow can be downright stupid.

"Let's tackle something a little smaller and simpler," Homo Sap steered the conversation like a canoe in a river. "Why do you still wear Western clothing in the jungle?"

"Because they are comfortable," I remarked, squirming on my bench, making sure that the multiple chafing marks were not visible. The marks were hidden, but my body language belied the veracity of my statement with every twist and turn.

"I wear what I wear, because it is practical," Homo Sap smiled trying to lighten the conversation. "If I lived in a cooler climate such as Canada, do you think I would be clad as I am now? No, I would be practical and wear what the local peoples wear to keep comfortable and healthy. Does being part of Western civilization mean you have to be impractical?"

"Of course not, but it helps," I managed a weak smile.

"For you, your clothing has become a symbol, an indicator; whether you are still who you are or who you think you are."

"I am a Westerner, a Homo sapiens," I desperately replied.

"I am not arguing your origins," Homo Sap stated gently. "But everyone changes. We are not discussing who you are, but whom you are going to become. You can never change your origins, but you can change what your attitude is for the present and the future."

"Impossible!" I declared, but nervously thought, "is this my irresolvable problem? My own opinionated view of the universe?"

"No, it is easier than you think," Homo Sap declared. "I am sure you are aware of the story of Alexander the Great and the Gordian knot. How the prophecy said the person who untied the knot was destined for greatness. Alexander took one look at the knot, took out his sword, and sliced right through it, essentially, unraveling as well as splitting the knot asunder. Your choice is like Alexander's. Take out your intellectual sword and cut through this entanglement of thoughts. Free yourself from your own prison!"

My sullen silence permeated the jungle. In my agony I was perversely comfortable with my Gordian mess.

"I have a suggestion. You have enough material to send in to your editor. Go downriver and send the material in!" Homo Sap broke the tension, but did not offer any magical assistance. "During the trip, you must make the decision on whether you want to return. This decision to return is the hard part, but you have to make a deal with yourself that once that decision is made there is no going back, no regrets. I will even make this easier for you. If you don't return in ninety passages of the Sun, I will hide our river from you forever and you will never be able to return no matter what you do. So, even if you don't do anything you will be making a decision."

"My editor probably would like some stories," I admitted. "I could use a break, and Perky is looking to get away also."

"Sometimes the fool sees what the wise man cannot." Homo Sap patted me on the back as he prepared to leave. Although I thought initially the Noble Savage was making a deprecating statement referring to himself, I later wondered if his last statement was a commentary on Homo saps and Homo sapiens, also. "So, don't be afraid to be a fool."

Following this conversation, I immediately began preparations. Within two days I was ready to depart. I was not necessarily happier, but at least I was moving again. I had a plan of action. I had activities that took my mind off Silesia.

For this trip, Homo Sap did not stir the water for me and Perky. We went arduously down the Orinoco without his assistance. The trip took us only 22 days (I say 'only' as my back is killing me), since we were following the current; this gave both of us plenty of time to put in some thinking.

About 10 days into the trip, Perky started going crazy saying he wanted to go back. If there had been two canoes, he would have taken off on his own to make it back to the Noble Savage and his tribe, but I was DETERMINED to complete my quest. (Perky knew what I was like when I was determined and provided no resistance.) I would send in these articles regardless of how many times Perky jumped out of the boat saying he would swim back. After each of these episodes, I would remind him of all the nasty creatures in the dark water that would either eat him or infiltrate his body in most unpleasant ways, and he would somberly climb back into the canoe.

Eventually we found a small village, from which I was able to wire all the stories and photographs that had been collected to the newspaper. Perky wanted to take off, but I would not let him take the canoe, and the native guides somehow had been instructed not to help us. How? Bird-speak, I suppose. Perky agreed to wait seven days, but he was adamant that on the seventh day, he would be in the canoe on his way back with or without me. I remember him vividly stating "I'm not going to take a chance on being late!"

Then, I sat and waited in a dusty old hotel room, thinking again when I should have been making decisions. (One thing I was decisive about was to create a new will with a local lawyer and send it to my lawyer in the states. Somehow, my trust in Roger had fallen by the wayside, along with his presence in my will. The terms of my new will put my niece, Eva, as beneficiary, allowing her or her descendants access for educational expenses only.)

I had taken a marvelous journey for the sole purpose of seeing what I could not see. Now that I was seeing and feeling new sensations, I was changing and this changing made me afraid.

I was like a child going to school for the first time. I was simultaneously excited and scared to death, but then I had my parents guiding me and assuring me and putting me on the bus.

As I entered this process of change alone, I needed to guide myself and assure myself. I had to become the hero in my own story and find the courage and wisdom to go beyond what I once thought I was. I was learning what happens meant to me, but I was still hesitant. Is this all there is to me, to life? Wasn't I much more mysterious and complicated or was I simply a love-struck idiot?

I was on the edge of my pursuit into happiness as new questions rushed forward. Was I having an epiphany about the relationship between Silesia and me? Had I finally left denial behind me? Any sudden jolt could propel me into the infinite ether of love. Fortunately, this contemplation did not last too long, when a wire came back from my editor:

> Stop. Where is the story on UFOs? Stop. Don't come back without it. Stop. Your editor.

Sometimes the answers to tough questions come from the darndest places.

Discussing Trined Gods[7]

The Editor had sent me back again (or did I run back with delight or dread?) into the untamed jungle in which lived the Noble Savage, living among a people who had been previously untouched by civilization until Perky and I had come upon them a few years earlier. Apprised by bird-speak of my imminent arrival, Homo Sap had sent a contingent of guides from the village, clothed only in blue, insect repelling paint, to meet me. This made the journey back a lot easier. They were waiting patiently on the other side of a quaking quagmire. Silently, with back-swept arms, as was their native custom, they bowed their greeting to us. The leader motioned for us to step forward and come across the almost invisible, moss-covered rocks, which were the only safe, though perilous, passage between them and us.

Perky was ecstatic to meet his friends from the tribe and with the unthinking fearlessness of youth, Perky, first ran across to their side, shouting ribald greetings to them in the local vernacular. I understood enough of the language to know that the epithets Perky and his comrades were bantering would make a *melona* blush. Then he came back to my side to help me toss our equipment over to the guides, bounding gleefully after me as I crept slip-sliding over the stones. Teetering uneasily I took one timid step forward, then another, until with a gasp of prayer and relief; I was finally standing on solid ground by them.

The guides led us forward; their sharp-edged bolos ready to slash impeding jungle growth, careless of the thorns and spikes of the repellent vines and fronds before them. I swear that as fast as the brush was cut down, it would spring back to full growth behind us. The sweat was running down <u>my face and neck</u>; although the misty air was damp and hot, my tongue was dry with thirst. It seemed days, not hours, before we broke into the clearing wherein the Noble Savage tribe was domiciled. Relieved, we spotted a jackal-type dog baring its fangs in a ferocious grin of warning at the sight of us. It growled deep in its throat. I stepped back in dismay, but my photographer cheerfully wandered over to the bristling creature and patted its head with a playful "Hello, doggie, longtime no-see", which instantly turned the animal into an affectionate household pet.

Although my editor had provided the impetus, I realized that I had made a decision. So, the first thing I did once I was back at the village was to find a loin cloth. Fortunately, this clothing was easily obtained and I was outfitted quickly. Although feeling a little awkward, I then went out to find Silesia. I scoured the *compong*, finding her fishing in the small river that passed by the village. She had seen me approach.

"Gud mo-orning, Norman," the English words were coming a little easier for her. "Ow can I 'elp you?"

"I have come to help you practice your English." I stated as confidently as I could.

You can not imagine how happy I was to see her, and she had no doubt about my happiness. (I should have worn my baggy Western clothing!) This is where women have an advantage over men, they can conceal their emotions better, but for men they shine through, sometimes embarrassingly so, especially if all you have on is a loin cloth, but Silesia seemed to be happy with my response. The practice went well, although English was a much smaller component of the exercise than I expected.

Later, Perky and I went to a large tribal gathering called a *beltane*, in which the women danced and the men talked (and watched). Homo Sap beamed warmly at Perky and me, indicating that we should seat ourselves by the fire, which was lighting up the darkening clearing, for it was now well past sunset. (Ooops, Silesia and I had spent the whole day together! According to the Noble Savage's logic, Silesia had been taking advantage of me all this time.) The flame's dry heat was strangely refreshing as it dried the sticky perspiration that ran down our faces and dampened our clothes.

Comfortably in the buff (except the loin cloth, of course) and as innocently indifferent to it as Eve (and perhaps Adam) in Eden, I watched as the females of the tribe were coming forward with pleasant smiles and gourds of delicious fruity liquid. Although the colors of their insect repelling paint varied from woman to woman, I averted my eyes from the sight of their luscious bodies, keeping them strictly on the gourd from which I was quaffing thirstily. (If I looked at Silesia especially, I could not trust what my body would do among this company. I still had to work on my puritanical hang-ups.)

After the dance completed, the women urged us to take our fill of the exotic foods and fruit they spread out for the evening meal on a woven mat of reeds before us. This was the first time that Silesia sat down beside me so that we could eat together. I started to wonder why it took me so long to get to this point and I felt somewhat betrayed by my basic assumptions. (Modern society is perfect? Savage society is a crude shadow of what a real society is about?)

My photographer greedily set to and gorged away on whatever he could reach. It never ceases to amaze me that, although he always eats as if he'd not had a bite to eat for a week, he never seems to gain an extra pound! (If I were to indulge like that, they'd have to use a crane to lift me into a ten-ton truck. I'd never be able to get into an ordinary car.)

At another encouraging grin from Sap, I smiled back, but felt uncomfortable when he asked me what brought me to visit him this time, as if he didn't know the answer already. Not able to be honest with myself, I clung to my Editor's demand for a UFO story, but I was hesitant to bring it up, so I brought up the touchy subject of religion. (Is this another mark of civilization? First, I could not be honest with myself and then I could not be honest with my dishonesty. I was still clinging to some civilized traits. Silesia will beat that out of me soon enough.)

"Is it possible to get some clarification on the differences between the beliefs of Western Civilization and those of your world?" I asked deferentially.

"The Ed wants-ta know what kind of Voodoo you ignorant aborigines practice out here. Do you perform human sacrifices? That kinda thing!" My uninhibited photographer blurted out. For a moment, sending a fulminating glance in the young man's direction, I could have made a living sacrifice of *him* at that moment, but I kept my twitching hands off his throat (I shot a searing glance at my cameraman that clearly told him, "Get out of my sight, you numbskull, go play with the other kids, before I make mincemeat out of you.").

Amused, Homo Sap had intercepted our silent exchange, but merely said, "The young are so abrupt. Still, they cut right to the kernel, don't they?"

"Er, yes," When Homo Sap laughed, amused, not angered, I began to relax. "If it's not too much trouble—not that I want to intrude on your sacred beliefs—could we discuss them?" Stuttering, I assured my host. "I will understand your reticence in such a personal matter as your faith, if you would rather not talk about it. My Editor will be disappointed, of course…"

"Maybe in the future sometime, but I fear that you are not ready to partake of our sacred teachings, as of yet." The Noble Savage shook his head.

"If we could discuss the tenets of *your* faith, I could describe my beliefs and indirectly you can get a glimpse."

Perky coughed in the background.   Relieved at the Noble Savage's understanding, I decided to let Perky go.

"Why don't you go take some pictures of Flora and Fauna, Perky?" I suggested strongly and gave a relieved a sigh when my unhappy photographer understood and took my veiled proposal.

"Gee, thanks, Boss," The young man's bright eyes twinkled back, as he joined the other younger people at play. I shot Perky a glance that said you're off the hook, but he was already gone.

"Let me draw a chart for you," I gathered myself, picking up a stick and drawing a diagram in the dirt. "This will be about the various religious pantheologies in the history of my people: the Phoenicians, the Egyptians, the Greeks, the Romans, the Teutons and the Celts, ending up with the Hebraic version of Genesis.

The Noble Savage looked on fascinated by the notes and my imperfect diagram. This is what I drew in the sand, jotting notes on the side.

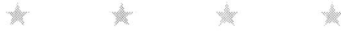

☆   ☆   ☆   ☆

Some Trinities:

Rome:

> Idea: Jupiter m., Hera f., Alma f.
> Moon: Luna f., Diana f., Dianthus m.,
> Sun, moon, dawn: Phoebus m., Phoebe f, Eos f.

Greece:

> Sun, m.: Apollo,
> Moon f.: Cynthia, Hecate, Selene

Germany:

> Sun f.: Die sonne, ––
> Female Trinity: Heaven: Asgard; Hell: Hela and Earth

	England	Germany	Egypt	Rome	Greece	Amerind
Idea	God, the Father	Odin	Ra, fathered by Osiris, his son	Jupiter, slang for Deus pater	Zeus, or Zeus pitar	Great Spirit
Spirit	Soul, Madonna, Holy Ghost		Isis	Alma	Hera	Old woman
Male	Man, father	Sol	Osiris	Apollo	Phoebus	
Female	Woman, mother, Moon, Earth	Sonne, Hela of the Under-world,	Isis	Juno, mother of many gods Luna	Hera, mother Cynthia figure	
Material	Solid	Water	Air	Terran		

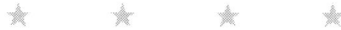

☆   ☆   ☆   ☆

When he had finished reviewing this rough summary, Homo Sap said, "Hmm! Most of the ancient religions in Europe and North Africa appear to have trined and twinned their god or gods."

"Er, yes."

"All of them were trying to reconcile the eternal question of how something came out of nothing or something returned to nothing."

I couldn't disagree. At times I still asked myself the same question.

"Although the Egyptians had a unique perspective, It is easy to see how generally Earth came to be worshipped as the Great Mother of all, for without apparent pattern, she seemed to create life everywhere, with or without males, from coral in the sea to water breathing animates, then air breathing land creatures and the stars that blossom in the sky."

I nodded mutely.

"It is easy to see why the primitive peoples came to believe in the divine qualities of water, Sun and Earth. Without water, nothing in the sea or on earth could survive; without sun, no life could flourish in the deeps of the sea or the sky. But, above all, none of the creatures in the sea, sky or land could take physical form unless Mother Earth chose to give them existence—an existence which she could just as easily refuse or terminate."

"Earth is not a goddess," I retorted. "Neither is the sea, the sky nor the sun."

Homo Sap grinned that infuriatingly mocking smile of his, and I angrily plunged into the nitty gritty as recklessly as Perky. "Sap, do you believe in God, or do you not?"

He pointed to the now starry heavens, for while we ate and drank, the world had finished its circuit from the light into the shade.

"Of course I believe. Look up into those purple depths; at the many stars like ours, each possibly with one or more planets and, sometimes, orbiting those planets, a moon or moons. Only a fool would think that such a complex, infinite design had been drawn up without a plan by some great organizer, some great Idea. One of your religious cults refers to this plan as the Intelligent Design."

I pretended to nod wisely at Sap, as if my college majors had been physics, astronomy, cosmology and religious philosophy instead of anthropology and my degrees meant something out here in this jungle wilderness.

"Could be," I added my non-committal reply. "On what grounds do you see this?"

"The usual three."

I raised my brows inquiringly. "Another trinity? And *you* see those as–?" (I felt I had used inflection in the word 'you' very cleverly, to pretend I knew what Sap was talking about. I didn't, but I pulled out my pad and pencil, turned on my pocket recorder and acted as if I did.)

"The Idea, the Spirit and the Sensitivity," the Noble Savage quietly listed.

I still didn't know what he was talking about, but acting the part I said confidently: "On what basis?"

"Can you see a thought, your own or anybody else's?"

I had to admit I couldn't.

"Then how do you know it exists?"

"Because I exist and feel it, see it in print, or hear about it."

"Aha! There you are. Did not one of your great thinkers say, 'I think, therefore I am?'[8] Is not the corollary to that, in this space and time, I feel, I see, I hear, *because* I am?"

"Ugh, that's quite a different way of putting it," I stammered.

Homo Sap gave a positive denial. "Not really. As you have just shown me, Man throughout the ages here on Earth has viewed the creation of the world and all its creatures in this three-fold way. Look at the gods in your recorded past, the Phoenician Baal, the Egyptian Isis, or Nordic Hela, Greek Hecate or the Romans, Juno and Jupiter, as well as Cynthia, Selene or the Celtic Brigga."

---

8   René Descartes, 1596-1650; of course, with the question mark one wonders if this quote is still Descartes or the Noble Savage.

"How can Baal, Isis, Hela, Hecate, Juno or Jupiter have any relation to the deistic aspects of our time?" Using inflection again, now *I* was confused.

Homo Sap said, "Quite easily, even today, their ideas, especially those of Egypt's Isis, Osiris and Ra color your thoughts to some degree, especially the relationship of male and female to the universe."

"What do you mean?"

"For thousands of years, men worshipped the mother goddess Dana as the Idea, the eternal spirit and creator of life on Earth. The serpent, with its tail in its mouth, was the symbol of her exaltation. Then they learned that animal life could not be triggered in the egg—as a rule—without the male's sperm. At that point in time males began to denigrate the female in flesh and spirit, even to claim her as an evil force, but they still had to account for the fact that, if an invisible force existed, how was he to be born into visibility, without a female force to assist him either into heaven or the flesh. They knew that females of all the creatures about them, including humanity, could bear children of either sex—and sometimes children, who were hermaphrodites. In order to be born at all, men had to have a mother. So, men saw themselves subject to Mother Earth, calling her Dana, Hera, Juno, Madonna–whatever you like."

The dance had largely subsided and the people had scattered to a number of smaller groups around campfires. Our originally large fire had died to glowing embers, orange eyes peeking out of the black dust of ashes. I listened in silence as Homo Sap put some more wood on the fire and continued.

"When men began to understand the part they played in conception, they still had a problem." Homo Sap continued. "How did this invisible force create man, if no man existed? The Earth was always there, solid and visible. The Sun was not. It rose in the morning and died into nothingness at night, until reborn in the morning. It was also obvious that Nature and all the creatures on it were dependent on that sun for nurture. Having given birth to a male, did that same male impregnate Mother Earth, so that she could give birth to other males and thus produce all Mankind? After all, the existence of Earth is just as mysterious as that of the sky with all its galaxies. Only the Earth, it seemed, was both spirit and flesh. The sky was not. Somehow this nothingness conjoined with the spirit of Earth in a bodiless, therefore immaculate, conception, producing a son capable of mating with Mother Nature, thus engendering the masculine element. Men have always recognized this trinity as a seeming fact of the nature of the cosmos in which they live. At first, they tended to exalt, and later to sacrifice (or both) the messenger above the message"

"I don't get it."

"Did not your prophet Moses say that one of the Ten Commandments is: 'Thou shalt not kill'; yet you sacrifice, legally execute or kill in His Name in unholy or holy wars? Yet this message in the *Old Testament* clearly stated you should do otherwise.

His messenger or prophet, Jesus of Nazareth, also said all souls are equal (male or female) in Heaven, but you make a Hell on Earth, because you elevate one man over another, this nation over that. As followers of Dana, woman over man, and in modern religions, man over woman. One of your God's most recent messages came via Jesus of Nazareth, who said, 'Love ye one another'. But you only love those, whose love is expressed *your* way, whether in race, politics or religion. All others are slighted, abandoned or eliminated in many sad ways."

"As for a messenger, like Osiris, in order to demean the Mother Goddess, called Isis in Egypt, Osiris, her son, had to die and be turned into Ra, the great invisible creator, to father himself, through Isis, as the son."

"This trinity?" I gasped.

"Yes, of course. Every god that man has ever made is twinned and trined. In Greece, the sun's twins are Phoebus and Phoebe. Its trine is Phoebus, Phoebe and Apollo. Most human faiths have some kind of holy trinity: the idea, male or female; the spirit or life, male or female, and the Sensible (male or female) in a world where flesh is solid. The Egyptians worshipped the holy trinity of Ra, Isis and Osiris, father, mother, and son. But their trine is incestuous. Osiris, as Ra, conceived his son, Osiris, with Isis, basically making himself his own father. For how else could it be until Osiris was born?"

"Osiris is his own father? That's weird! No wonder the Egyptian Pharaohs were into marrying their own sisters, since this represented a pattern of cosmic creation in their religion. But, how in reality can this be?"

"Possibly because the scenario is, symbolically, a kind of death and resurrection, and partly because man, having discovered his part in the miracle of birth, wanted to replace the Feminine as both the physical and the non-physical force behind the cycle of eternity represented by the female snake with its tale in its mouth."

"It represents infinity," I proudly reminded him, "the other name for timelessness."

"Yes, but it also exalts the female as the prime force in the creation of man, as can be seen in the varied myths retelling the origin of man."

Puzzled, I remarked, "I still don't get it. It's only the representation of a circle, and a circle is a pretty good way of picturing time, which has no end. Looks sexless to me!"

"It also represents the circular mouth of the uterus from which physical life springs, male or female," Homo Sap pointed out. "Men don't have wombs as a rule, only the occasional hermaphrodite."

"So what?"

"It's obvious. As soon as men learned the importance of the male contribution in the conception of the next generation in all nature, great and small, including man, on Earth, in the sea or in the air, they wanted to exalt the male as the chief creative force in this universe."

"Everyone knows that males are stronger than females throughout most of nature," I remarked loftily.

"Bees don't," Homo Sap stated dryly, "neither do spiders."

For a moment I was stumped, then retorted, "Like hermaphrodites, they're only anomalies in nature."

"I doubt there are any anomalies in nature. These exceptions may also have a most important reason in the continuance of nature, which man does not yet understand."

"Still, without males, what life could there be on Earth?"

Homo Sap chuckled. "Oh, there could be life, but you wouldn't like it. The lowest forms of life just split themselves in two, to increase their populations. And that sexless, or perhaps totally female, life existed before masculinity appeared on this Earth, a masculinity that could not perpetuate itself except through union with femininity."

Totally perplexed, I asked, "But what has that got to do with Isis and Osiris?"

Patiently, as if talking to a child too young to grasp essential concepts, Homo Sap said, "Don't you see? By making Osiris father to himself, husband and master of Isis, the Egyptians, were trying to abase the female Mother goddess to a place lower than the male gods in the cycle of creation here on Earth."

"Even so, that is not true of our *Genesis*," I defended.

"Why, then, do you suppose, vengeful Adam, to prove his mastery crushes the symbolic serpent, representing woman, beneath his heel, or that Eve is made the criminal in man's fall?"

"At least WE haven't twinned our God" I wasn't sure what to say, but plunged into speech. Belatedly I remembered Satan, but avoided mentioning that fallen angel. "Who or what being is the object of *your* prayers?"

"My tribe prays to one Great Spirit, who, in every aspect, reflects the trinity of Creation, or Idea, the spirit and the sensibility in all nature, throughout our universe."

"Oh, no," I gasped, "That's Pantheism. That isn't so in *my* faith. We pray only to one God."

"What? You have no Holy Father, Mother and Son? Are you sure? Have I not heard of prayers reverently picturing Him in a holy trinity of the *Pater, Filio, et Alma,* that is to say, the Father, Son and Holy Ghost, where Alma is the female spiritual life force, the *anima* behind the Ideal Father and His Earth born son?"

"You insult our faith by your comparisons," I declared angrily. "We do not belong to any of those outmoded cults."

"Of course you don't," Sap agreed, "neither do we. What I am saying is that no matter what our rites and customs, most of mankind believes that there is a great invisible Creator-Ruler of the universe, who, in one person embodies every component of the solid, the sensible and the bodiless animate force, which empowers the cosmos we see around us. Since our human eyes and minds can neither see nor feel nor comprehend it, that 'Good', or 'God' as we call it, is defined by each faith, and their definitions can be used to measure how close each religion is to the true reality of God. You may be sure it is not a true depiction of the Great Idea if its worship engenders harm to, or exclusion of, anyone, male or female, young or old, whether of its belief or not. A true Good, or God, hurts no one. He made us all; He is our Father (or maybe our Mother), and, like any good parent, no matter what our faults, God loves us all. His punishments will not kill thousands or millions for the wrong doing of one, although in our own stubborn ignorance or defiance of the natural laws of this planet we may release plagues that do destroy many of us."

"Even other faiths?" I growled. "Intelligent design, for one."

"Why not, since it is an admission that objective science is more likely to bring us knowledge of the nature of the spiritual universe than arguing from factual ignorance."

On Music

The jungle hummed and buzzed and squawked. Alligators bellowed in the reed-choked river. Mosquitoes and gnats zinged against my eyeglasses. Some creature shrieked in the treetops, and a loud mewling like a tortured cat added to the pandemonium. In the distance, colorful birds argued with each other. The constant croaking of the frogs on the water lily pads throbbed like a drum roll in my head. The locusts added to the racket and three tree frogs added a soprano counterpart to the deep throated baying of a doglike jungle beast. Sweat rolled into my eyes and clouded my glasses. The humidity was high enough to qualify as hot water.

"How do you stand it?" I gasped, fanning myself with a *percoolar* leaf—it looks like a rhubarb stalk but it isn't. Unusual warmth had pervaded the rain forest. The Noble Savage raised his mobile brows questioningly. Taking a finger and wiping the sweat like a sheet of water from my brow, I raised my voice and yelled louder, "HOW DO YOU STAND IT? ALL THIS RACKET AS WELL AS THE HEAT?"

"S-s-sh!" Homo Sap put up a finger to his lips and leaned closer to whisper, "Don't interrupt this section. These particular jungle sounds are the basis for part III of the *Symphonia Jungeliana*, by Moe Kingberd. A-a-ah!" he sighed in ecstasy at a particularly raucous outburst.

I gaped at him in amazement. This hellish noise was music? Was Homo really a sap? Was he crazy? Sweating and wiping in huffy silence, I waited until a lull in the volume brought him out of his sound induced trance.

"What do you mean those screeching whining, thrumming, drumming, bellowing noises are MUSIC?"

He looked at me in surprise. "Has no one ever related the saga of *Semper Vita* to you?"

"Never heard of it."

"I suppose not.   Come, let's sit down by this pool among the *farron* fronds and cool our weary feet." He pushed aside some waving stalks of what looked like fern to me, pressed them down into a cool mat. Surreptitiously, I put my hand down and discovered that it was much cooler close to the earth; so when he sat down, thankfully, I followed suit and did the same. (Well, heat rises, they say)

I got out my note pad. My editor would be interested in the discovery of a hitherto unknown aboriginal saga. *Semper Vita* sounded like some melodious archaic title for a tale from the tribe's mythological past.

"It is related in the *Semper Vita* –you can read an English transcription of it by an obscure Professor Emeritus in Massachusetts[10]—in which God made Adam and Eve, because Eternity was so lonely, and He had no one to talk to but Himself. Every virtue has a vice and God's shining virtue has an opposite darkness, but since together they make an omniscient whole, even from darkness can good come forth."

"Ah? Massachusetts?" I hesitated; this did not sound like an aboriginal tale to me.

"During the years when God was preparing His children to handle the fullness of knowledge, the songbirds were silent, because the only sounds they could make were hissing whispers. They envied the beautiful voices of the sky, the earth, the animals and insects that made music in Eden, from the bass of the rumbling water making harmony with the wind; the soulful baying of a wolf at the rising moon running counter to the constant shrill beat of the cicada and locust, the basso of the frog. They did not complain, for that was how it was, had always been. So they listened in silence as Eden and its dwellers rejoiced in their being."

"God was still lonely, for His children were too young to talk to Him. His loneliness was like a diamond scaled serpent, twining around the Tree of Knowledge. His thoughts were music in the feeble minds of lesser creatures, but to Man, they were as speech, which their own human desire translated into words they later claimed the serpent had spoken. Each species of the envious birds heard a chorale of musical sounds they longed to voice."

"You know how Adam and Eve were tempted, and how they shared the Golden Apple," Homo Sap said.

---

10   Nora M. Barraford, Professor Emeritus, Worcester State College.

"Everyone knows that and we have discussed them before," I grumbled and started to close my notebook. I realized now that the Noble Savage had not been reciting some obscure tribal myth, but *Semper Vita*, a Latin term meaning 'life forever'. My editor would be disappointed. "This is no great twist to the universal myth of creation. What about it?"

"Do you remember what happened to the snake?"

"The snake?" I reopened my pad. "I don't recall anything happening to the snake."

"Well, Adam was pretty angry. He hacked the serpent into two parts. He stamped on the tail part and shouted, May you crawl silently forever in the dust and dirt, you ugly, treacherous thing!"

But the head flew into the fork of a tree, and a bird swallowed it. When trying to dislodge the object choking it, the bird emitted beautiful sounds that God realized were missing from the Heavenly choir of Nature, so He exchanged the voices of the birds for that of the serpent, and transformed the latter's shattered hind into a body, which slithered away into the jungle, hissing. Now, the delighted birds fly all about helping nature's choir to make the only sounds like God's upon the Earth. In their human efforts to represent God's voice in music, all musicians throughout time have imitated them."

Homo Sap quoted the following verses from the *Semper Vita:*

> Behold! Now could speak the voiceless bird
> Its mellifluous voice that of the singing serpent,
> Emblem of the sad side of loneliness,
> And all birds since are mellow tongued
> With such sweet music as must represent,
> The only sounds like God upon the Earth.
> Thus the lowly crawling snake contributed
> Its instrument to the elephantine trumpets,
> The drumming hooves, roaring tidal beats
> And clapping thunder of Nature's symphony...

When he finished, Homo Sap said, "Do you see now? All noise is music, and every instrument or engine you make can be used to create a musical picture of the world around you. Music is only noise arranged in patterns that take your fancy."

"That's a fabulous tale," I protested, "but the twittering and squawking of birds is still just a racket to me."

"Of course," Homo Sap agreed. "Since all music is noise, it is the arrangement of that noise which makes it into music for your ears. The sound of an engine, the roar of a plane, the clatter of horses' hooves, the bellow of a bull, the squeak of a door, the cry of a child, every sound is noise, until a composer turns it into music."

"Okay," I said wearily and bowed unwillingly to his greater wisdom. I thought of songs including the sound of a train, of the trumpet blasts in military music, of the plaintive crooning of a Brahms' lullaby and had to agree. Music is only noise arranged in patterns that take our fancy.

The Noble Savage Cites Aesop[11]

I had gone into the deeper jungle to let off steam and I was screaming at the monkeys, when Homo Sap stumbled inadvertently upon me. I didn't even have my cameraman with me, because I didn't want to endanger my plush job, by having interested ears hear my heated remarks and, directly or indirectly, have them used against me politically.

Homo Sap was a patient and silent ear. I almost counted him as an old friend, so this coincidental meeting was fortuitous. (I have wondered since, if anything in Homo Sap's life is accidental.)

"Homo Sap," I yelped, "I'm scared to death about my sister's children. The sons of our country are out there now, facing enemy gunfire on the front line in the desert. My niece will be next, I know, helping to clean up the mess when the battles are over. How could my favorite Prez[12] do this to me?" Hands over my face, I wailed in my hands, mumbling about the cost to the country in lives and armaments.

Homo Sap looked puzzled. "But didn't you tell me that this was his personal private war? That he started this by himself?"

"Sssh!" I said and looked around warily. Could the trees hide an electronic bug? Do satellites have ears? I cautiously stammered. "Er, yes. He didn't ask the UN. He unilaterally declared war. It's going to kill our nation's children and eat up our country's assets, paying our soldiers, moving them around and making their armaments."

"You told me once," Sap heedlessly continued, "That he was so rich he owned eight castles. Isn't that rich enough to have his own private army and pay his soldiers himself? Can't he house and heal the refugees and prisoners

11   April 11, 2003
12   George W. Bush Jr.

117

as well, pay the widowed, the orphaned, and the crippled he has created, himself?"

"But then he'd be poor, and we taxpayers would still be left with the bills for cleaning up the mess. We would still be left with the muddle he's making in the desert. The bad credit and loss of faith in our country all over the world will ruin our reputation as well as our trade! We'll be morally and economically broke, too."

Homo Sap shook his head sadly. "Too bad you humans never studied the fables of that great philosopher, Aesop," he murmured.

"I've heard of him," I grumbled, "what's he have to do with this situation?"

Homo Sap laughed. "If all of you had heard the story of Jupiter and Mrs. Bee, you might not be in this situation."

"So?" I countered, and ever the sucker, added, "Go ahead, spill it."

"Well," Homo Sap began, settling back in his hammock, arms folded comfortably beneath his head. "Mrs. Bee went to see Jupiter one day. She was in a buzzing fury about some intruder who had been robbing her stash of honey."

"That Neddy Gnat and his thieving pal, Teddy Bear," she was buzzing furiously. "I'll teach them a lesson, I will!"

"Jupiter," she hummed, "will you do me a favor?"

"Sure," he muttered absently. He was checking the accuracy of his lightning bolts.

"You promise?"

"Of course! Didn't I just say I would? You know I never break my word. What do you want?"

"Give me a sting so deadly it will kill my enemy with one thrust."

Jupiter looked up worriedly. "You're sure this is what you want?"

Mrs. Bee buzzed aggressively. "Of course it is! Remember, you promised!"

"Okay," he sighed. "You have your sting."

As she flew off triumphantly, Jupiter called after her, "I hope you remember to use it wisely, Mrs. Bee, and be sure to control your temper when you do; if you don't, the recoil will destroy you, as well as your enemy."

As I mulled over this fable, puzzled, Homo Sap added: "You know Jupiter was referring to the fact that when a bee uses her sting, the force pulls the stinger out of her abdomen and kills her too. Wielding power is dangerous – for the wielder. The initial thrust of power is no problem, but the backlash can be a killer."

Who is the Sap? Homo or I?[13]

"I don't care what they say! It's in the *Bible*. A circle is the symbol of eternity. So a circle is a circle, no beginning, no end." I blurted out, and Homo Sap nodded his head. The jungle man did not seem in the least upset, even when I told him my fears that the scientists were trying to destroy God by breaking *His* circle.

"I don't think you read that in the *Bible*," the Noble Savage remarked, offering me a woven dish filled with chopped sugar cane. I took a piece, automatically. "Of course," he went on thoughtfully, "it depends upon which translation and language you were reading. Was it from the scrolls, the *Septuagint*, or an earlier one of the seven Greek versions of the *Bible* or one of the later Latin versions, the *Vulgate* perhaps, or any of the many English versions of both the *Old* and *New Testaments* since the King James edition? Remember, the *Bible*, both the *Old* and even the *New Testament*, were first passed around by word of mouth—certainly the *Old Testament* was an oral history, perhaps for hundreds, maybe thousands of years before being inscribed on parchment scrolls. Who knows how many storytellers had put their slant on the *Old Testament* before the Hebraic scribes began to document it?"

"Similarly the various accounts of the events in Jesus' life by the 12 apostles were passed about by word of mouth until, some years after Jesus' death; they were collected and written down in Greek, still the common language of North Africa at that time. Certainly they were edited by each scribe to reconcile the twelve varying accounts from the viewpoints of twelve

---

13   From his jungle fastness, the "Noble Savage", unspoiled by Man's Institutions, offers His Circumlocutions 'about the Eternal Cycle of the universe', as reported by a local resident for the world at large. Saturday, 10, 2001

different men. (Or more, if the apostle were dead and his account was written down from recollected hearsay.) In general, the events of both the *Old* and *New Testaments* do agree on certain major events and sayings, but who knows what was actually said or implied originally? A man is prone to exaggeration or downplays, or even lies, if it suits his purpose. It is true a day of judgment is prophesied, but to end Eternity...?" Homo Sap shook his head. "I doubt that's possible," he responded frankly.

"You do?" I felt a slight relaxation of my tension. Why do I let myself get so worked up? It's bad for my blood pressure...

"Think a bit. To exist, a cosmos must contain elements of idea, of motion, perhaps emotion, to power idea into action. A cosmos of nothing— no action, no reaction, no idea—is impossible, because, were that true, there could be no such thing as existence or of God at all. Personally, I don't think God *can* die."

("He's crazy," I thought loftily, but then, he doesn't have the benefit of an education like mine—I have a graduate degree, and once I even took a language course at Harvard University! He's only an ignorant jungle savage. However, I am a tolerant person and generously make allowances for his outrageous beliefs. If he saw one, he'd think a college campus was the tribal site for a big *beltane* gathering. Next thing you know, he's going to bring up one of those oldies of his, "How can you have an UP, if you don't have the DOWN side of electro-magnetism—the non-metallic, fat-and-dirty side?" You know! Then he would laugh like a hyena at his own jokes.)

I jerked myself back to the present.

"So consider," Homo Sap was now saying, "a universe of total non-existence is doubtful, because a universe exists, and we exist in it. On the other hand, while a universe of eternal static something might exist, without the driving force of Idea or Intelligence to push its atoms here and there, such a universe is also doubtful. However, the universe we live in is not static. It contains motion, sensation and the powerful impetus of an Idea; an Intelligence that is a Creator, visible or invisible, for where there is motion, there is time. Where there is time, there is a beginning and an end—"

"That's what the scientists are saying," I anguished.

"Of course, but you aren't thinking clearly. There is no end as you envision it," Homo Sap continued calmly, "have you never considered that whichever way God turns His wheel, every point on His cycle is the end of the road and the beginning of a new one, a never-ending spiral up, down or sideways in every direction?"

"I know that," was my sour answer. ("Who's the sap here," I grumped inwardly, "Homo or I?") He stood up and with one of his loud guffaws, gave me a comradely slap on the shoulder. But my mood brightened, as I said excitedly, "You're right. Every end is a beginning, every beginning an end, but all ends are open, because, for God, time doesn't exist, and, Man has free will."

Homo Sap finished, "Man can shape to some degree, the direction of the path on which he'll pass through his own life—up, down or around–"

"But he makes his own mistakes—" I offered.

"Yes, and as usual blames them on God," Homo Sap finished, "just as Adam passed the buck to Eve, blaming her for their fall from grace. He knew he couldn't pass the guilt to God at that time, although he has found ways to do so on many occasions since then. Man hasn't changed much, has he?"

More on Science, Circles and Cycles

Homo Sap and I had returned to the magnificent waterfall without Perky. (Somehow I was relieved to be not responsible for the young man.) I had asked Homo Sap to return to the waterfall and clearing, because I yearned to get a clear view of the sky. Arriving at night, we had settled in the clearing that we had camped at previously.

Before I went to sleep, I watched the stars twinkle through the humidity, but at least I could see the stars. This morning the magnificent blue sky was totally clear, while the earth below splashed and bubbled, sometimes majestically in the far distance and sometimes not, like a little stream that seemed to dance across our clearing, providing us with water and music. This reminded me of a small poem I once had come across:

> Gurgle, gurgle
> What is this?
> Little stream
> Distilled from mist,
> Singing soggy
> Lullaby
> To frogs and fish
> And drizzly
> Sky.
> Gurgle, gurgle

What is this?
A little stream
On a sparkling quest.

What was my quest? Why did I need to get out from the pleasant green shroud of the rain forest and to a place where I could see the sky? I settled myself down for a chat with the Noble Savage.

"All these physicists are not only trying to make us believe that the eternal cycle of God's Being is not forever, that eternity has a beginning and an end." I groused, keeping true to my self-image. "Some woman called Rao is asserting that a *muon* can tell where the end is and change the direction in which it is spinning. Almost as if the dam' thing could think!"

"Oh, you mean that study at the Brookhaven National Laboratory," Homo Sap stopped chewing on his sugar cane stalk long enough to reply knowledgeably. I gaped at him. (Bird-speak seems to get the news out into the wilds faster than a telegraph.) "What about it? So, once in a million times, there was this fluke. A *muon* reversed direction."

"A fluke? Don't tell me that. There may be flukes in the human universe but not in the heavenly cosmos!"

"Then why are you so worried about it?" Homo Sap responded reasonably. "How do you know this deviation from the 'Standard Model' isn't a planned action? After all, I can roll a stone; you can roll one of your wheels, backwards and forwards or in different directions. Surely God can do as much with His circle?"

"I suppose you believe rocks are alive, too?" I said sarcastically.

Homo Sap raised his eyebrows in surprise. "Don't you?"

"Yuk! You do think they are animated." I grabbed the last piece of sugar cane before Homo Sap reached it. Almost didn't get it by a finger width–Sap can be fast, even though he is the laziest man I know. At least he practices what he preaches.

"Why not?" Homo Sap asked. "After all, rocks are composed of atoms, just as we are. Their subatomic particles are busily spinning away to keep them what they are, rocks, just as ours cling together to keep us what we are, human beings—though sometimes I have doubts about our humanity."

"Maybe you are right," I reluctantly agreed with Homo Sap. "But while the scientists were measuring the spinning of the *muon* particle, they claim it reversed once in a million times. Is this natural for subatomic particles? I'm no physicist, but doesn't it conflict with the standard third law of physics or something?"

"It is a possibility that the *muon* or any other subatomic particle may be sentient."

But anger—or was it fear?—still rankled. I've been mostly a vegetarian for years, only eating an occasional lobster because they were killed so painlessly, because their armor, a scaly exoskeleton, prevents them from feeling pain. That was my understanding, until some know-it-all woman reminded me that from head to toe, we are scaled creatures, too, (we call our scales 'scurf', 'dandruff', and 'dead skin'. Girls use skin peeler lotions to get rid of the dead scales on their faces), and we could feel through our scales, couldn't we? When I gave a defensive reply, the cruel creature ordered me to put my cup down—we were having lunch at the time—and put out my hand, which I did automatically. The heartless creature put a drop of scalding hot coffee on my thumbnail. I almost screamed with pain... I squirmed uncomfortably at this past memory, and asked, "If everything is alive and can feel, what can we eat?"

"Nectar and ambrosia, like the Greek gods," Homo Sap gave one of his slyest smiles.

"Nectar and—?" I raised my eyebrows interrogatively.

"Curds and whey, too, the same thing Miss Muffet was eating when along came the spider and sat down beside her and frightened Miss Muffet away!"

"Sour milk?"

"What else?" Sap guffawed.

Honestly, I don't know why I keep letting Homo Sap set me up like this... Well, maybe it's because I like the Sap, no matter what kind of outlandish things he says.

"Aren't we getting off the topic?" I said peevishly.

"You're right, so what do you think about the *muon*? Do you think it's a sign that God's machinery is out of kilter?"

"That cannot be. You said yourself that God created the universe and everything in it, so He must have created the muon, too. Sure, if God makes no mistakes, any that we think we see, must be an indication that the man-made machinery used to make that sighting is inadequate or out of kilter. Or maybe the *muon* did change its mind about its direction at God's desire—or the physicists have learned something new about what was already there, which will enhance their views and widen their scientific knowledge. Our universe is, after all, only God's university where we can learn or not as we please."

I was so shocked; I dropped my piece of sugar cane. A dozen ants swarmed over it. They like sugar. "Are YOU saying that a *muon* is equal to God, that, like Him, it can alter the physical laws of the Universe?"

"No. YOU are saying that. All I am saying is that anything is *possible* to God, and, if, at any time, He wants it to be that way, the *muon*, or any other subatomic particle may be sentient." Sap continued. (Apparently, Homo Sap still believes in the out-dated law of opposites. Dualities, you know. As

I reported earlier, he says things like, "How can you have an UP, if you don't have a DOWN?") "Except in the sense that, like us, they are part of His Universe,"

"Then what are these things, these *muons?*" I questioned.

"I don't believe *muons* are God." The Noble Savage declared. "Do you think you are better than God, because, like Him, *you think, therefore you are?* All I say is that a *muon* may be sentient, that it may *feel*. I don't know whether it thinks. And I do believe that just because it is tiny doesn't mean the *muon* can't feel as many *dukkhas*[14] of pain as you do. Small or large, as an old African woman once said, 'If your cup is full, it is full...' It doesn't take much thinking for some one or some object to be thrown off course when slammed into a barrier. But if, occasionally, such a barrier exists, the *muon* may be proof that there is indeed no end that is not a beginning. The possibility even exists that you could go back in time and start over. I hope so. If I could take my memories back with me, I'd welcome the opportunity to straighten out my own mistakes. In a one way only world of chance, this is impossible, but in a world directed by a Universal Intelligence, which can make its own laws and even allow one tiny molecule to make a difference, perhaps by its actions on the molecules around it, to alter the universe, to live again may be a possibility—or even to go back and discuss matters with one's previous self."

"I would!"

Homo Sap fell into a pensive silence.

"Though I can see why God hasn't given this ability to everyone yet. Suppose, without changing his crazed, paranoid outlook, Hitler could have discovered *his* military mistakes; and then gone back to correct them and conquer the world?"

"Good God!" I gasped. Surely there should be the crash of rumbling thunder as God stamped His feet in anger, the flash of lightning when His eyes blazed with passion! But the jungle around us was gripped in sultry silence. Not a flower swayed, nor a palm frond waved. Deflated, I thought, that maybe, as Homo Sap once wryly observed, God doesn't ever get angry. Maybe He cries because we are so stupid...Or maybe Earth is really Hell, and Death our redemption, or extinction–depending on our conduct during our life sentence in the durance vile we have made of our planet.

"Good He is, indeed."

"I can agree that if we knew more, we could be wiser," I reluctantly admitted.

"Knowledge of anything in the universe isn't wisdom," he warned. "Wisdom is the ability to use science or anything we know for the good, not

---

14   "Dukkhas" is a word coined by Ralph Siu of the Panetics Society meaning 'measures of pain'.

just of ourselves, but of all God's creatures. Not only must we humans learn to live in peace with each other, we must learn to live with all of nature and not destroy God's balance. Take away the buffalo and the prairie will vanish into forest. Take away the predators and, the buffalo having over-eaten the prairie, will die, too. We must learn to live together and share our prairie, our kindergarten world, our earthly university with the lesser creatures. Indeed," Homo Sap averred. "The more I think about it, the more the world in its travels about the sun, voyaging on its own path amid the stars in its galaxy, itself only one among countless millions of galaxies in a firmament of forever, looks more like a puzzle to me, which God wants us to solve."

"That is a big puzzle," I pondered.

"The biggest!" Homo Sap smiled with agreement. "Because of our scientific curiosity, our constant querying into the known and unknown, we have made remarkable strides, from the eggbeater on the kitchen counter to machine-made planets, satellites, reporting galactic events from outer space. What is science, after all, except the constant questioning of our own theories? Maybe science's search to know more about everything we see or think we know, always hunting for better answers, is the way to the resolution of the universe's mysterious existence and our place in it. There are clues everywhere, which, right or wrong, we must examine before the true picture revealing His Presence, falls into place. So, if the *muon* does occasionally reverse direction, it may be the best proof yet, that *God exists*, and that He can, indeed, change His mind and His direction, in regard to the universe, as well as of His creation, Man".

The Noble Savage looked up at the azure heavens, and then at the area around us, filled with gloriously colored vegetation, where we were having our discussion.

"We aren't the only beings or things He created, you know." Homo Sap added.

I experienced a feeling of connection with the sky and the trees and the sparkling little stream, a feeling that I had never felt before of being part of a larger plan. This union of myself with the unseen stars and galaxies, the Earth, even the un-seeable *muons* spewing forth from the mists of the rivers, made me realize that I was originally disconnected. My civilization drove me toward a state of alienation where I was detached from the largest to the smallest vistas of the universe, not to mention my own human kindred. This epiphany fulfilled my quest for the day, as I searched far into the past and future.

Grinning, I darted a mischievous look at Homo Sap.

"Does that mean in a few thousand years, our snooty descendants will look back at us and sneer they couldn't possibly be descended from apes like us, no matter what the evidence of our fossilized bones seems to imply?"

"This is Good," the Noble Savage simply stated with a smile.

Darwin's Theory of Evolution

"Now they're saying that Darwin's studies on evolution are only an outdated theory!" I yelled in jubilation, as I got close enough to Homo Sap to speak to him after I entered his *compong*. One of the women winced at the raucous sound of my voice. Another covered her ears with her hands. Perky, who had rushed ahead of me and was standing among the giggling females, yawned. Having been subjected to my harangues about this subject on the way here, he quietly scraped the toe of his boot in the turf. Perky isn't into this stuff; he didn't need to take biology in his college as a requirement for his degree. He began to edge away with an increasingly 'Why get so excited–This subject is so bo-o-oring?' look. I dismissed him with a frown. One grateful glance and in seconds he was engaged in a weight-lifting contest with a group of laughing young men, starting with the smallest 'weights', little girl toddlers and moving up through teen age girls to the heaviest of the women, a pregnant woman, whose massive girth and delightfully plump breasts seemed to indicate that she might be carrying twins or triplets.

"You were saying—?" Homo Sap gently reminded me. My attention caught by the game—Silesia was taking part in the fun, which captured more than my attention—I had lapsed momentarily into silence. With a jerk, I returned to the subject.

"They are saying that evolution is only an out-dated theory now." I could hardly hold my satisfaction in. I was NOT descended from an ape…I was NOT…"

"That is good science," Homo Sap answered approvingly.

"What do you mean that is good science?" Expecting strong disapproval of the unorthodox notion, I was taken aback.

"Well, isn't it? Science is built on theory. Someone postulated the theory when he saw lumps of sand on a beach, burnt into crystals by volcanic heat, that if he could take some sand and heat it enough, he might be able to make throwing stones out of it—or marbles to play with. Other men saw what he was doing and made further postulates on what they saw him doing; maybe they could make a fake sea shell to hold the marbles in, when they were playing with them and made glass. Maybe a woman watching the men at play saw a better use for a fake shell—to carry water from the brook for every one to drink, instead of making ten trips by carrying it to her children in her cupped hands, and household utensils were created. Other men may have wondered if they could heat clay instead of sand, because inland sand was hard to come by and the fragile glass vessels shattered into shards so easily. Thus a new industry, pottery making, was created. Later ores replaced sand and clay. Smelting metals allowed man to form even more durable, copper, gold, and iron objects as well as alloys like lead and brass. Eventually someone thought up a better way to heat the substances used and open fires were abandoned for closed furnaces. Then, as more scientific information became available, even the fuels used for the heating evolved. Coal replaced wood; oil replaced coal; electricity followed, and the metal, glass and porcelain factories evolved into the giant industries they are today. But the nucleus of their evolutionary theory remained the same. If you heat certain substances, they become malleable. In the same way Darwin's theory has itself been altered now as humanity learns more about its own past. But you don't throw away the old theory entirely. The world has gained a lot from Darwin's discoveries. Besides, he never said we were descended from apes; he said they, like us, were a lesser branch of the same hereditary tree—and DNA proves that they share man's inheritance."

"Don't tell me you think we descended from apes!"

"Alright! I won't," he replied, his eyes twinkling merrily. "However, you have to agree Darwin's theory of evolution did help us to understand some of the otherwise inexplicable changes and variations in the land, sea and Earth creatures on this planet, including man, which, from ages past, man has been struggling to understand. As we came out of the dark ages, remnants of past knowledge survived, which had not been destroyed by the righteous fury of iconoclasts, like those who threatened Galileo with torture and death if he did not give up the round Earth theory for the simpler, mentally short-sighted, flat land theory. (Why, anyone with eyes could see that the Earth was flat!) This theory gave succeeding scholars an opportunity to move man's knowledge of life on Earth a further step forward. Virgil's comments on cattle breeding in the *Bucolics*, Galileo's beliefs about the nature of this planet's position in astronomy, and the expeditions of Columbus and the

Portuguese, all led to newer theories about the creation and evolution of the entire cosmos, the galaxies, the stars, the solar systems, the planets, not just of plants, cows and men."

"These scientific questions about evolution and other proofs are based on Darwin's travels around the world, as well as Alfred Russell Wallace's local and accurate observations. Other proofs came out of the minute and detailed experiments on and observations of several generations of plants by Gregor Mendel. Plus the discoveries of the fossil remains of early man were the most scientific proof of our earthly beings' descent that science had ever had a chance to put together. All over the world God has created, fowl and cattle breeders have made use of Mendel's dictates on heredity to improve the size, fertility, egg and milk production of their flocks and herds, as well as the hybridization of corn and peas."

"So you do believe that man was descended from the apes," I accused, disdainfully. "I believe in Intelligent Design."

Homo Sap laughed gleefully. "So do I. Sir James Jeans himself said the universe was a great Idea. Do you not believe in God's intelligence?"

"But you just said that you believed in evolution," I stammered.

"Of course. That is the nature of *this* world God made," he pointed out, "And because of Adam and Eve's flight from Eden, **we** have to live in it. How do you think we could do it, if God hadn't fitted us into the earthly pattern of the creatures that could live on Earth?"

"So you do believe we are descended from the apes."

"I didn't say that at all. What I am saying is that, bit-by-bit, science is helping us to find out the nature of this world into which Adam and Eve exiled themselves. With the ethereal bodies they must have worn in Eden, how do you suppose they could have existed in the three dimensional world to which they had exiled themselves? God knows all, both past and future. Don't you think He must have been prepared for such an action on His unruly children's part and given them a physical entity when they came here that rooted them into the ecosystem of this world? We may not yet know where He placed us in the evolutionary chain, from which the present human form descended. Certainly there is no biblical description of the human shape or form while in Eden. But it was, and still is, very necessary that our physical human selves fit into the natural system of this planet and share its creatures' abilities to alter form, size or color in order to survive until our time-out here on Earth is completed. Our exodus from Eden may not be as close as we think, or it may be much, much further back. (*Considering the fishy arguments of some of our politicians, the swinish behavior of some people, could be worse than a tiger's ferocity and cruelty of others; it does make one wonder if our species deserves to belong in the relatively decent order of apes. Certainly it doesn't belong among such a gentle, playful genus as the dolphin.*) As a kind of punishment to fit the crime, the Intelligent designer, the Great Idea, may have placed His little monkeys among the apes to make us fight our way forward into the superior beings we once were—or might have been, had we not been so indifferent to God's wishes."

"On the other hand, any breeder of birds or bees or animals, any student of biology or geology, recognizes that if our earthly physiques could not adapt or alter to their planet's environment, whether for what we would see as better or worse, we would be doomed to extinction as a species here on Earth, which I don't believe is God's plan, even if He has to turn us into rodents who must fight our way forward into noble primates. I believe that God, that most Intelligent Designer, is allowing us, through our scientific studies, our constant questioning of everything on heaven and Earth, to prepare ourselves to move out into space in search of suitable planets to live on should our own Earth show signs of becoming a nova before He thinks we are ready to return to Eden."

"Ridiculous! The Intelligent Designer would never do that!"

"Well," Homo Sap said pensively, his lips pursed thoughtfully, although the twinkle in his eye was devilish, "Since you know so much more than God does about His Designs, why use Darwin's and Mendel's theories of heredity to determine the relationship of a child to its parent by checking its DNA? As for me, I bow to the great Designer and try to learn more about His wonderfully intricate designs every day. I can't even use the atoms in a lump of clay to turn my statue into a living thing."

"Do you believe in God or not?" My tone was acerbic.

His eyes glinted mischievously. "I am withholding absolute belief until all the facts are in."

"What do you mean?"

"What better way to prove there is a God than to try and prove there isn't? Keep those scientists hard at work. Look what they've discovered about the *Bible* so far?"

The Return to Eden

The dratted puppy peed on my best suede loafers, and I kicked it aside. It yelped and whimpered piteously on its way back to its pillow under Homo Sap's hammock.

"The saints will hold that kick against you when my little Damocles here gets to the pearly gates and tells St. Peter on you," the Noble Savage admonished. He reached down and patted the trembling little creature consolingly.

"Dogs don't go to heaven," I muttered peevishly. "He's ruined my best shoes. They cost me damn near five hundred and fifty dollars." Unthinkingly I dried them with my best Irish linen, shamrock green hanky and belatedly realized that it would be a casualty, too. High price or not, its color ran.

Homo Sap gave me a skeptical look.

"Are you certain? I have it on the best authority that all the animals, including man, were created in Eden, and that we treated them so badly, they will do anything to get even with us. Didn't they drive Adam and Eve out of Eden?"

"You can't get to Heaven without a soul. Animals don't have souls."

"I wouldn't be too sure about that. I'd say you'd better watch out how you treat animals—especially one of mine. I might get all upset about it. Really upset!" Homo Sap remarked sternly, with a menacing glare in my direction (he can look quite formidable), before he bent down and stared into the puppy's soulful dark eyes. "Hi, Damocles, what do you say, little feller? You alright?"

The little dog crouched against his master's leg and whimpered as it turned its pathetic eyes to me. I shifted uncomfortably as I stared back into its innocent little face. For some reason, I flashed back to a nightmare I once had. The dream occurred a few nights after I had surgery performed for the removal of my gall bladder several years ago. Despite the sedatives supposed to keep me comfortable, I was still in great pain, although barely semi-conscious. Eventually, I drifted off into another world. I thought I was dead and had gone to heaven. A long bearded angel with a glowing halo was showing me the sights. He led me up to a gnarled tree, with wormy, half rotten fruits.

"Here is the Tree of Knowledge," he pointed to the apparently dying tree.

"What's happened to it?" I said. "I thought it was supposed to be beautiful."

"Adam fouled it with his staff when he tried to pluck the fruit. Every apple he hit had a bruise on it. But as man recovers his innocence, the tree will improve."

"What do you mean about man recovering his innocence?" I asked, brightening. (Maybe here was another saga that might get me a raise from my editor? Even in my drug induced delusions within a dream, I am thinking about my tyrannical editor, Ed!)

"Well, man has to patch up his past before he can improve the present and the future."

I laughed. "Man can't change the past. I can't change my past from up here, can I?"

"No, but you can alter your feeling and thinking about it."

"What good would that do?" I scoffed.

"Maybe nothing," the angel agreed, "but maybe it might change the future."

I laughed. "My future or the world's?"

"Maybe both—"

I was astonished. "Those are mighty powerful words. That's impossible."

Now the angel laughed. "Anything is possible where God is concerned."

"Don't hit that poor beast!" I yelled over the wall without thinking down to a man on Earth, who was beating his horse. I couldn't believe he really heard me, yet he stopped the horse and got out of the cart. He went to the horse's head and patted it on the nose. Surprisingly, I could feel the kindness in his pat, his sudden remorse, could hear his words echo in the horse's head. "Sorry old fellow, we'll climb this together." The farmer took hold of the horse's bridle and helped the animal pull the load slowly up the hill. The horse whinnied and quickened its step. I wanted to turn away from the sight of man's further cruelties, but the bearded angel's arm over my shoulder made me totally immovable. I was forced to view a parade through the centuries revealing cases of man's inhumanity, not only to man, but all his fellow creatures. I was forced to endure every slight and blow I had ever given another creature in my lifetime, and I sobbed bitterly. The splendor around me had turned to black ashes and the glowing Tree of Knowledge was a gnarled and rotten stump, the withered fruit hanging on its leafless boughs, now wormy, pitted and rotting. All of Heaven had turned to Hell—a Hell I had made for myself.

I turned to the angel.

"I can't bear these sights," I said. "If this is Heaven, it's worse than Hell."

The angel nodded his head. "As it is for all of us up here, who are redeemed, or are working to redeem themselves. This is where you pay for your sins," he said. "You are going to be very busy amending your share of the past." He pointed to the battered tree of knowledge where a single tiny bud was sprouting. The bearded angel shivered.

"I have made that journey. I don't want to make it again. This job is hell enough for me," he winced, grabbing his mid-section with one hand, the other to his jaw, as I now viewed two angry men exchanging blows. Feeling the same pain in my own diaphragm and jaw, I winced, too, and shrieked, "Tell God I'll do anything—anything!–to relieve any agony my sins caused on Earth!"

"Done!" the angel promptly said. "It's a deal. See that pitiful beggar? You can allow the vicissitudes of his life to fill you and see what you can do to better his life and those of others. To assist and guide you in this endeavor, God will give you empathy to the pangs of others. You will feel their agony as if it were your own."

"It won't change what happened, for that is history on the scroll of time. For example, after WWII—" Snapping back to current reality, I saw that it was Homo Sap, not the bearded angel speaking to me.

"But how—" I started to ask dazedly, shaking off the memory of my dream. I wondered how I could have forgotten or tried to forget such a vivid dream and, belatedly, I regretted kicking Damocles.

"For example, after WWII," Homo Sap ignored my obvious disorientation and continued. "Your country realized that punishing the grieving and distressed of the conquered only led to further war and bloodshed, as well as worsening the battered economy in both countries, so, after WWII, instead of crushing Japan, they tried to make peace and help them. The net result was that they became friends and prosperity bloomed for both countries. But you must make the choice. God won't."

"Why not?" I asked, amazed, and found myself fading back into my dream.

"Because God won't give pain to anyone. If you went back, you'd have to take the body of a cripple, a deaf mute, a mentally impaired person or some other unhappy creature, maybe an insect, a fish, a horse, a hungry orphan, an abused child, a woman, a beaten slave, a criminal facing execution. You might be born to poverty; you might be born with wealth and power, perhaps a prince or dictator. In all cases, animal or human, you will suffer severe physical or mental pain. Born innocent, you would have to re-make your own path, ignorant of why you were on Earth, until the task your presence will alleviate is over."

Shuddering, I remarked sheepishly, "Your words remind me of a nightmare I once had," and related the angel dream to him...

When I finished my narration, Homo Sap did not laugh. He merely nodded with understanding sympathy. Sometimes Homo Sap can be so nice, it's aggravating.

He cleared his throat. "Your angel had a valid point," he agreed. "Even Heaven *will* be Hell for anyone with a conscience, until mankind makes Earth an Eden full of joy once more."

"And those without a conscience can burn in Hell," I growled. I lost my favorite uncle in battle, and some crook crippled my only brother with a single shot in the spine during an armed hold-up.

Homo Sap laughed at my display of temper, then said thoughtfully, "Oh, I don't know—I think a worse punishment would be if God gave them a conscience and lots of empathy to feel the suffering of others as you did in your dream. Make the punishment fit the crime, as Gilbert and Sullivan remarked in one of their operettas. Was it *The Mikado*? Heaven must be Hell to its inhabitants as long as Man is making Hell on Earth. I feel sorry for those tenderhearted souls up there. How can any heavenly being find pleasure in Heaven as long as Man is making a Hell out of Earth?"

For once I fully agreed with Homo Sap.

His words brought my dream back to mind. Was there some kind of an answer to that heavenly problem in his words? Must we make a Heaven down here on Earth, before we can expect one upstairs?

On Metamorphosis[15]

Happily stretched out in a hammock near Homo Sap, I watched the antics of the young, including Perky, dancing barefoot about an open fire. The blaze was there, not for heat, (the jungle was torrid enough, although it did make the heat more bearable by drying the damp jungle air about it), but to perfume the air with aromatic wood—with the added benefit of its scent repelling invaders of all kinds from insects and reptiles to carnivorous animals—as much as for its friendly illumination.

I sighed. Reporting on this tribe was my cover, but it was also my living and helped Perky payoff his college loans. The lad hadn't a clue about the true nature of Homo Sap's people. He believed them as innocent as they seemed. So I again broached the question of whether Homo Sap believed in evolution or Intelligent Design.

"Both," he answered promptly.

"But how can that be?"

"It's quite simple," he averred. "There is no void; no absolute emptiness and complete stasis. We know infinity *is*, because we live in a cosmos ruled by an organized, ever changing, deathless animation, both with and without material form. Order suggests *idea*, or Intelligent Design; just as animation suggests feeling and emotion. Change may occur from accidental, that is evolutional, causes, with resulting change or changes. It may also occur, using nature's basic substance, as a farmer creates a better or new species from mutation, from accidental or planned changes. Ergo, evolution on higher

---

15   Homo Sap does not answer the question (which science, as well as man in general, seeks so diligently, and whose findings have helped us in many ways – in some instances even to find God – so I say, let's keep the scientists on the job and praise their efforts when they find a new 'truth', until further study finds it is an untruth or part of another greater, unfolding truth): Why is there ANYTHING, unless a great Idea exists? How can anything come from nothing? N.M.B.

levels, Intelligent Design, may result either from godless chance or from heavenly personal bias."

"You've been reading those books about the da Vinci Code or the one saying that Christ never rose from the dead," I accused.

"Speaking about Christ, you're jumping to conclusions," the Noble Savage said reprovingly.

"Oh, yes! Perhaps one of your ancestors was one of the Magis following that star." I suggested sarcastically; my sarcastic emotions told the story that, maybe, I did not believe it.

"Everybody followed the stars, on land as well as at sea. No roads or handy signposts back then; if you didn't watch the stars at night or the Earth's star, Sol, by day, it was easy to get lost in a forest or a desert. But you are quite right," he agreed amiably. "One of my remote uncles *was* in on the whole thing. It was a kind of victim/witness protection deal between the Romans and Christ's father and brothers."

I gaped at him. "What do you mean? The whole thing was a set-up? I don't believe you."

"You don't have to take my word for it. The clues are right there in your history books," he asserted.

"What clues?" I asked stupefied.

"Well, you know that Joseph, his father, was a member of a wealthy, highly influential Jewish family. Joseph, himself, seems to have had widespread interests, stretching apparently from what is now Israel as far as Egypt. He appears to have been on good terms with the Romans. Many Jewish people were, although there was a rebellious far right Hebraic group, constantly threatening the political *status quo*. That group obviously regarded Jesus as a religious dissident, and an enemy to their extreme orthodoxy. Pontius Pilate was trying to preserve the tenuous peace in the Middle East, and the trial of Jesus was forcing him to make a decision, which would further that idiomatic schism or start a major outbreak in the area. So he washed his hands of the matter and turned the case over to the quarreling sects. You know what their decision was—and I'm sure there were plenty of followers of Mars and Mithras to swell their ranks. After all, Jesus was a threat to those, and many of the other ancient religions. He changed the world. However, according to my long ago uncle, his assertion about there being one god only. This was quite shocking to the Pagans everywhere, depending on sacrifices to the Earth goddesses to keep their crops and herds multiplying! In addition, Jesus' revolutionary views that the souls of men and women were equal in heaven, brought him into conflict with some of the Jewish middle and upper class as well, which meant—"

"I can't believe this," I muttered repetitiously.

"That his family and the Roman government must have had to plot secretly between them to get Jesus out of this mess?" Homo Sap continued. "I assure you, such political maneuvers were nothing new then, nor are they without precedent today."

"The Romans hated him so much a Roman soldier gave him vinegar to drink instead of water," I insisted. "And then they stabbed him in the gut with a spear."

"No, quite the opposite," Homo Sap shook his head negatively and remarked wisely. "If the Romans had really wanted him to die, they would have ensured his inability to survive, if he did get away. It was the custom to break the knees of violent criminals before they crucified them. To start, they did not break Jesus' knees. They either liked him or were in league with his family to save him, and that drink proves it."

"How?" I demanded.

"When Roman soldiers were on the march, they drank vinegar and water, not only to conserve their supply of that last-named liquid, but to prevent dehydration of their body fluid and resulting loss of strength. In this case, they may have slipped a narcotic into the mixture that caused him to become unconscious and therefore appear dead. The stab in the side was a mercy cut, in a way. It could cause you to die sooner and therefore save you a lot of agony. It would also ensure that you were really dead when they cut you down from the cross for internment—better than being buried alive, too."

"There, you see," I exclaimed in excitement, "He really did die and rise again!"

"Could be," Homo Sap agreed, "but on the other hand, his family might have bribed the centurion to draw blood, but not kill, the newly comatose, doped man on the cross."

Crestfallen, I nodded and said reluctantly, "I see what you mean. Could be a stab in a usually lethal spot, but the thrust was just deep enough to draw blood and *look* fatal."

"Exactly! The Romans were highly professional soldiers and they knew precisely what it would take to kill or not kill. Then the grieving relatives cut him down from the cross and bundled him away…far, far away, as far as their money could take him—after his apparent resurrection. This was a path that could have killed Jesus, but it looks like a gamble all parties were willing to take to get Jesus into this ancient witness protection program. (In this case, Jesus was a witness to the word of God.) To further distract matters, one of his brothers took his shroud to Turin; another took the Holy Grail to Avalon, from whence it disappears, and is subsequently pursued by King Arthur's Knights of the Holy Grail. King Arthur's mother was a Roman you know, as was his uncle Merlin."

"I suppose you think that Jesus made off with Mary Magdalene and lived happily ever after in some idyllic corner of the Roman world."

"Possibly, that would be a nice, romantic and happy ending to the story…" Sap was non-committal on the outcome of Jesus' life.

"Well, I prefer to think he died and rose again," I growled.

"Not possible."

"Why not?" I argued.

"Because, Jesus was the Son of God, and therefore immortal: *he couldn't die*," Homo Sap pointed out. "On the other hand, as a material creature of the universe, according to those who argue that God does not exist, neither can you die. You can only change from one form to be resurrected as another. The living energy that is you, the invisible, immaterial thought that says 'I am', may not be lingering in the disintegrating material of your flesh, but it cannot die, either, even if it cannot communicate with those still in the flesh. What we call corruption or decay is merely metamorphosis."

On Getting Ready to Take Off [6]

Having been away at a neighboring *compong* to visit Silesia's parents, our party was hot, sweaty and tired from trekking through the tropical jungle; we paused after crossing the river. (I discovered women, Homo sapiens or saps, still operated invariably in the same way. First, determine whether the man of interest is worthy enough to keep around and then parade him in front of her parents. If the parental reports are favorable, the wheels start turning to entrap the poor fool who ventures too close to the flame.)

Drawing in a deep breath of the humid air, a faint smell of–was it sulfur—smoke—fire?—entered my nostrils. Lifting my eyes from my dusty boots and looking back at the river, where its wide sweep allowed a view of the distant mountains, rising darker blue over the distant tree tops into the darkening blue of evening, my horrified gaze encountered a small cloud of smoke spiraling from the thankfully still silent, volcano's crater.

My alerted senses became aware of unusual activity and raised voices from the tribal settlement, which was now not too far away. My conscience twanged. Were Homo Sap and his people preparing to take off to some remote hide-away, because my published articles in major papers had brought their presence to the attention of the modern world? Or, I thought, with another uneasy glance at that forbidding cone, was their activity a forced response to the signs of an impending eruption the volcano was showing?

Perky had eyes only for the treasured new digital camera he was showing off to his youthful companions as he made a pretense of focusing on the distant peak. (What a lot of energy the young waste, I thought indulgently, watching Perky duck and dive, waving his camera about to escape the clutching fingers of his pals, all eager to hold the new instrument in their own hands. What a pity we can't bottle it up for better uses at a later time!)

Turning back to face that menacing cone, I wondered if we were all doomed, Perky's precious toy included, soon to be overwhelmed by a river of boiling lava spewed from the volcano's fiery bellyful of magma? Another thought jarred me, as I remembered Homo Sap's vague threat that if the modern world got too close, he, himself, was going to start up an eruption to scare away modern man. I sucked in my breath.

On my first visit, Homo Sap had hinted he could—or had he?—control the volcano, but until I saw that curling white cloud emerging from the volcanic crater, I had never been able to get up the nerve to ask him outright how he could do that. Sure, I have my share of brass, or gall, where people are concerned, but without it, I could not have lasted long as a newspaper reporter. Even for a reporter, someone who claims he can move mountains (if he really can!) can be a wee bit intimidating.

When Homo Sap saw me and waved me to come over to him, I made a now or never resolve out of—or into?—the blue, to ask him forthwith about his peculiar semi-warning, semi-threat.

"Are you blowing up the volcano?" I asked excitedly.

"No," Homo Sap responded absentmindedly. "Just getting ready to take off in a spaceship."

"Spaceship?" I shouted. "A UFO?"

"You don't have to shout," the Noble Savage admonished me.

"Earth isn't really your home?" I stated in a much calmer voice. "That so-called eruption you once spoke about isn't really an eruption, and you aren't really of this Earth, although you say you are human."

Homo Sap did not deny it.

"No," he admitted, "My people haven't had a permanent home on Mother Earth for many years. We have only been here on a temporary basis for a mere 5000 years."

"Why did you come? Where do you go?" The questions were coming fast and furious. "Is this humanoid form your true form?"

"Yes, but, in fact, your Disney science fiction animations of monsters in space amuse our children greatly. Most parents find it amusing, too, to watch their children pretend to be the extra terrestrial monsters you think we are, but some parents are concerned about the bad effects that watching such violence may have on the emotional growth of their children and forbid them the use of their long distance viewers."

I ignored this slur on the content of our cinematic endeavors and continued my investigation.

"So this mountain's occasional rumble of what seems an impending volcanic eruption with a few attendant earth tremors meant to scare people away, is merely the result of your people's spacecrafts landing or taking-off?"

"Sometimes, if we feel such pretense is necessary," he agreed. "Our spacecraft are noiseless, landing gently as a feather, if we don't want to call attention to ourselves; we can be totally imperceptible to your modern radar installations."

"I see. Why do you come at all if you don't want to live here? Do you come to steal minerals or other substances from us that are valuable to you, but lacking on your planet?"

Homo Sap shook his head negatively. "You have nothing here that is of much use to us."

"Then why do you stop here at all?"

"Well, Earth is a kind of intergalactic rest stop and fuel base among other things," Homo Sap conceded with his wicked grin. "So we shall probably meet again. I like to use my vacation time, traveling from galaxy to galaxy, star to star, planet to planet."

"I knew it!" I gasped, affronted. "You aren't really human? You are an alien from outer space, and you are stealing our precious oil."

"No, you have it wrong," Homo Sap protested, "Don't get so excited. It's bad for your blood pressure and your clarity of mind, as well. I may have been born on another planet, but I'm not an alien species. I am as human as you are, even though the possibility exists that I've come here from outer space."

"That makes you some kind of alien," I averred. "Humans developed on Earth. Our ancestors were Adam and Eve."

"So were mine," Homo Sap said agreeably.

"You're lying," I protested. "You can't be. We don't have any colonies in outer space yet."

"If we were not somewhat human, Perky would not be able to procreate with us." Homo Sap smiled at my logical dilemma. "And that does not seem to be the case."

"I know Perky has had children, but I have doubts about his humanity anyway," I rejoined, "As I have about past human colonies in space. We have no proof."

"Not yet," Homo Sap announced, "But in the past you have had such evidence."

"What?" I stammered.

"Your *current* civilization hasn't had any proofs," Homo Sap said. "That's not to say that one of your long lost civilizations didn't. Anyway, what makes you think that Adam and Eve ever lived here?"

"They must have done," I fought my rampage of thoughts to get back into the conversation. (I do have to talk with Silesia. She must be an alien, too! Why did she not tell me? How many other secrets is she keeping from me? Argh! I've been making love to a space monster!) I was truly working myself up into a frenzy, as I responded weakly: "Eve ate an apple. Apples only grow on Earth."

"That may have been true once," Homo Sap shrugged, "but that's not to say some Galactic-traveling Johnny Apple-seed astronaut didn't litter space, or toss his chewed up apple-cores onto each planet he sailed past, including Earth, until all the Earth-type planets in this galaxy had an orchard?" Sap gave one of his raucous belly laughs. "Your Earth isn't the only livable planet in space, you know, and wherever Man goes, he takes his favorite animals, birds and plants with him. Look at this country. When the colonists came from Europe to America, they brought seeds, seedlings and cuttings of apples; pears, peaches, plums, oranges, gooseberries, raspberries, strawberries, turnips, cabbages, lettuce, celery, endive, parsley, onions, leeks and carrots; wheat, barley, oats, rice and rye; walnuts, peanuts, beechnuts, cows, horses, hens, ducks, white geese, domestic rabbits (America did have wild hare.), wild cats, dogs, donkeys, pigs, pheasants, sparrows, starlings, and pet birds like the Algerian dove and the canary, as well as such flowers as the lilac, rose, buttercup, daisy, dandelion, lavender, lily, and herbs like allium, bay leaf, ginger, marjoram, monardia—some people call it bee balm, turmeric, thyme and many others. It's likely our early colonists brought some of these to you as well, or took them back with them into space. That's what we do when we find a new planet. We terra-form it, as you say in your entertaining science fiction stories."

I was dazed. "If we came from outer space, how did we get here?"

Homo Sap grinned again. "That's easy. When we first developed a primitive type spacecraft many, many thousands of years ago, I fear we were as primitive as you people are, or at least as you were until the time of Queen Victoria. Our legal punishments were as gruesome, as inhumane, as yours were up to that time. Our people used to hang, but only to choke, not to kill; before drawing–that is, disemboweling–the criminal. Then, to accentuate the display, they finally quartered the carcass and hung the dismembered pieces over public doorways. Some people even favored tying each one of a living criminal's limbs to a different horse, then setting all four horses off in a different direction to dismember the criminal."

"We had become advanced enough to realize that executions and torture were not the way to cure crime or punish criminals. So instead of executing our wrongdoers in gruesome ways, we, like Queen Victoria and other reformers of that age, decided to give some of them a second chance in a new land. (Note: *Of four such young Irish criminals, Queen Victoria said they were too young to be the hardened villains the law made them out to be, and insisted they be given a second chance in Australia. All of them did well and became prominent Australian citizens. One eventually became prime minister of that vast territory. N.M.B.*) We had already sent explorers to Earth and determined it would support the life forms of our planet. It would be a great way, not only to punish the criminal in a more humane way, but to help colonize this, at that time, almost empty globe and expand our own empire. We sent them in gangs to live out their prison sentences of varying lengths on your planet."

"After completing their sentences, many chose to stay and build up respectable new lives here, because they liked the place. Some became fabulously wealthy and returned to their former homes in space. One of my ancestors was one of these," the Noble Savage confessed, "Some escaped their jailers and fled into the wilds to live and die on their own terms."

"Several of the civilizations these forced colonists built on Earth were truly remarkable, even developing space flight on their own and flying out to visit the planet that was the site of their physical origin. Unfortunately, because of such planetary or cosmic events as volcanic eruptions, meteoric or other cosmic collisions on your Earth, one of which actually shifted the axis of Terra's North and South poles, some of those civilizations now lie buried under Antarctic ice, at the bottom of the Gondolian sea, the deeps of the Atlantic and Pacific, or flying about as fragmentary intergalactic waste, no record or memory of their existence left except perhaps in your mythic tales of gods flying down from the heavens in thunder and lightning or tossing lethal thunderbolts about at will."

"However, after so many millennia, all history of their scientific knowledge was rapidly forgotten by your ancestors except for remnants in fairy tales such as the story of Aladdin and the stolen, vocally operated electric device, which opened the entrance to the cave of the forty thieves."

"Nearly every time one of your civilizations fell, you had to start again from scratch and rebuild afresh the technical knowledge that once had been yours." ("Your memories are not very good," he remarked aside, thoughtfully. "Many cannot remember the names of their first and second cousins or even their grandparents.")

"As our empire spread, we, your ancestral family in space, had similar problems, but were fortunate enough not to technologically regress. So as soon as we regained the power to enter space, we would send our emissaries out to do what we could to help others pull your shattered civilizations together. Many of our missionaries spent their lives here, married and had families, dying here after long, happy, helpful lives." He raised a speculative eyebrow humorously in my direction and interpolated, "*We get along so well together... Do you suppose we are more closely related cousins than we realize? I must do a little genealogical research when I get home—*," before continuing his explanation. "Others of our volunteer teachers weren't so lucky. Your ancestors regarded them as witches, wizards or magicians, whom you feared and burned at the stake—or put to death in other violent ways. Others you believed to be gods and worshipped. To some you gave a little more honor as prophets. Some of them were scientists and tried to give you knowledge, which you were still too backward and ill educated to consider. When these early pundits from outer space said the world was round; you said it was flat—that kind of thing. We never left you totally alone; we helped you as much as we could, or as much as, in your benighted state, you would allow us to do. Some of your early civilizations rose to such great heights, we were sure you would catch up to us, but alas, man's propensity to violence is so great that millennia after millennia, most of those civilizations were destroyed by war, never to rise again."

He paused, and I thought of Galileo. (*He* had claimed the world was round –had he been one of those missionaries?)

"You never quite forgot your past. Wherever on Earth a colony of yours has been settled, you carried memories of your beginnings in your legends, myths, epics and great religious works."

I nodded in agreement. All of the literature that Homo Sap was relating to stated that man had come from the skies, whether that place was Eden or another paradise, but still, there was the matter of that fuel, or other products that Homo Sap's people might be secretly taking from Earth to the skies, even if they were what he said they were, our distant cousins from space. Families are not always friends. Detectives always look for suspects in the family. Most murders, it has been said, are committed by someone known to the victim. We haven't always been on the best terms with the distant tribes of our closer ancestral relations in different countries here on Earth. Still aren't for that matter.

"With an increase in knowledge, there has been a corresponding decrease in energy requirements, we have found. We need a very small fraction of the energy you would expect." Seeing the renewed suspicion in my wary glance, Homo Sap smiled understandingly, "And no, we don't come to steal your bauxite, uranium or your precious petroleum. Although we do use Earth as a galactic rest spot, historic tour site and refueling base, we don't use those types of fuel."

Still suspicious, I asked, "Then what do you use for fuel?"

"Electricity," he replied matter of factly.

"Oh, then while you are here on Earth, you must use our wind and water power to make it."

"Once again, no," Homo Sap laughed, his eyes twinkling. "It's self generated."

Again I was at a loss. "Self generated? How?"

"If our personal power is running low, we rest in a sunny spot like this, so that the solar batteries of our spacecraft may re-charge in case of an emergency." A mischievous grin spread across his face, as he remarked solemnly; "No, what we use of your Sun's power is from the beams it is wasting in space when its face is turned away from Earth. Meanwhile our bodies build up an excess of electrical power. In this jungle the sunlight, the stimulating exercise of seeking and preparing our own food, swimming in the river, the complete relaxation of mind and body soon allows our physiques to regenerate any energy they may have lost. Depending on the number of passengers our craft may be carrying, some solar power may be necessary, but as a rule, all that is needed is a portion from each person of his own recharged, self-generated power added to the ship's regular batteries for the common cause."

"I don't know what you mean. Are you saying that your own bodies generate the electric power you use?" I said, still puzzled.

"With genetic surgery still in its infancy on your planet, I suppose you can't believe me," he agreed, "but, yes, our bodies do generate electric energy. We no longer have to depend on our planet's resources to power our machines. As long as we can find a pleasant vacation spot to help us refresh our personal charges, each of us can create sufficient extra energy for his or her individual uses."

"I don't believe you. That's not possible for any human being, let alone any other earthly creature."

"Of course it's possible. Your own brain already uses a kind of electric power to transmit messages among its neurons and so does at least one of your sea creatures, an eel,[17] Conger, Moray or some such, use an electric thunderbolt as a weapon?"

I was flabbergasted. "There is no such creature in our oceans." (Or is there? Ocean Biology is not my field, but a dim memory of such a creature rose in my consciousness. I must ask Perky to look up the electric eel—give him some practice in research—get him to put down that damn camera of his for ten minutes!)

---

17   See an interesting discussion and illustration on how a physical body might create or use electrical power in Patricia Sullivan's "Fill 'er Up, but Hold the Ketchup", pp. 24-30 in the *UMASS Amherst Alumni Magazine,* Volume 2, 2006. The Geobacter is a fascinating critter. N.M.B

"Yes, there is, and one day your people will be able to use your own inherent magnetic energy, too, as we do. All you have to do is find out how your planet's electric eel makes his thunderbolts and imitate his actions."

"Aren't you afraid I may tell the world about your secret source of energy? Bunches of secret agents might descend upon your vacation spot to steal your secrets?" I threw at him.

"No," Homo Sap responded jovially, "You won't do that because we are friends, and you want me to come back again and maybe give you a ride in my space buggy. Besides, if you did tell anyone about me or my people, they would never find us; we would dissipate like smoke in the night. People do not find the disappearing river unless we want them to find it. Worse, what would everyone think of *you* for believing such an outlandish tale?"

"All this talk about interstellar aliens, where are your ships?" I challenged him.

"Why, just over here," he waved as he brought me to the edge of a bog, where a brilliant oval shape gleamed over the bog beneath it. "This is one of the smaller ships, but it does carry 15 people."

"A UFO?" Stunned, I asked. "Is it taking off now?"

"Yes, it is leaving this spacetime shortly," Homo Sap confirmed. "But, this ship does not take off in the conventional sense. Three-dimensional travel requires a ship to gather speed to take off. Traveling *beyond* the three dimensions does not require speed; it requires the manipulation of time. So, when it leaves us, this ship will just disappear."

With a nod the ship in front of me did just that; it disappeared.

"Wait a minute, how do I know it wasn't a pocket of gas above the bog out there?" I thrashed through my boggled mind. "That could be a huge Will-o'-the-Wisp!"

"You don't" Homo Sap winked at me. "But now you have a story about UFOs for your editor."

"How did you know my editor wanted a story about …" I thought to myself. "That dratted bird-speak again!"

On Time

"Well," Homo Sap grinned impishly at Perky and me. "Now you have another world—or should I say star—shaking decision to make. Both of you have to decide whether you want to stay with us or go back to your lives in the United States."

"Do *I* want to be a Homo sapiens or a Homo sap?" I summarized quickly.

"I see that you have been listening to me," the Noble Savage nodded his head in satisfaction. "But, you can still go back to the United States and be a Homo sap."

"All I have learned is that I want to be with Biaka, and Biaka does not want me with anyone else!" Perky announced stoutly. Perky was quite a sight. He was tall and lanky, clad in a loincloth and painted with blue swirls and yellow suns. The locals painted symbols on themselves based on the local mythology, but Perky decided to paint random pictures, since he did not yet know that much about the tribe's mythology. When I asked him what the pictures meant, his answer was that he liked the colors and shapes. I believe that the tribal members decided to accommodate him and were making him and his body-art part of their myths, just to help him fit in. Perky had become a living myth. "I know what I want to do. Biaka and I have done a handhold or something like that, and she does not want me going anywhere."

"That's a handfast, Perky," I informed him. "In this tribe it means you are married."

"Whatever," Perky impatiently dismissed me, but his sense of certainty was disarming. The boy was grownup and able to make his own decisions, but his history of vacillation before and after his decisions stood in stark contrast with the maturity he was displaying in his current decision making.

"I have my last articles to get in," I prevaricated, the last vestige of civilization holding me back.

"I can help you with that," Homo Sap offered. "Bird-speak with a little bit of carrier bird-power will get the articles in to your editor and your sense of duty will be satisfied."

"I don't know," I still hesitated.

"Are you nervous about entering a deeper commitment with Silesia?" Homo Sap inquired, giving me a *man-to-man* tilt of the eyebrows.

"Not really," I answered serenely. "From a personal responsibility perspective, I have only three people that I worry about, my sister, her daughter and Silesia. (Somehow, Roger was no longer a concern of mine, surprisingly.) My niece became a surrogate child, but you know it may be time for me to think of having my own family. Also, my estate is already set up in trust for my niece, so I am not leaving her bereft."

"I didn't think this was making you hesitate. Your decision is not about going on a UFO and leaving, even though this *may* be a distinct possibility," Homo Sap calmly continued as if he were talking about fishing or some other mundane subject. "Your decision is whether you are going to be a Homo sapiens or Homo sap for good."

Yes, I had made the decision to come back and involve myself with Silesia. Despite the recent disclosures that she was an alien from outer space, I still wanted to be with her. (When I confronted Silesia with the fact that she was an alien from another planet, she stated "I am NOT a woman? Make love to me right now and then tell me I am not a woman!" Of course, being a scientist, I tested this hypothesis–immediately. My conclusion was that making love to an alien, well this alien, is just like making love to a woman.) The problem was more–subliminal. Hidden in the recesses of my brain there was a shred of civilization, which was trying to suck me back. Superficially, I had gone native, but at deep psychological levels I was a closet civilized man. Either I had to come out of the closet or shut the closet door forever.

"When you first came to us, being civilized was like a cocoon, protecting you from yourself." The Noble Savage reminisced.

"I was – different." I agreed.

"You came here disenchanted with this lack of–feeling–behind your life. It was like you were driving in one of your civilization's automobiles. The journey was interesting, but you never had a chance to taste the reality behind the ride. In a canoe, you can hear the water passing beneath the boat, feel the water splashing on your skin as you row, and smell the various bouquets of the jungle, some pleasant and some not, but the point is that you can experience the trip, the bumps, the bruises, the anguish and the ecstasy."

"I was not happy, when I came here." I recalled.

"To your credit, you have tackled the issue of happiness," Homo Sap smiled, almost proudly. "You realized that civilization's approach to the idea of happiness was keeping happiness away from you as a reality."

"I know I am staying here, but I do so with some regret and apprehension." I admitted.

"You need to shed some further baggage," Homo Sap declared.

"What are you talking about?" I surprised myself. When I first met Homo Sap, I would say something like this and it would come out shrill and defensive. This time, I was sincere and open and curious; I was entering a new stage of my changing life process, as I was becoming aware of the changes as they happened.

"Do you want to be a slave to time and property?" Homo Sap asked. "Or do you want to be the master of your Universe?"

"That's a pretty pretentious set of questions," I challenged, but with a smile.

"When you were back in your civilized condition, do you have to be at places at certain times?"

"Why, of course, yes," I stammered. "I have appointments all day long."

"So you have to abide by the constraints of a clock to maintain your dignity, correct?" Homo Sap explained what I obviously could not see.

"Yes," I admitted.

"And you do all these contortions for property," Homo Sap declared rather confidently.

"I do have house payments, car payments, even though my car is locked in a garage." I admitted. "Insurance payments, utility bills…"

"You are enslaved by your pursuit of property," Homo Sap interrupted what could only be a longer litany of obligations. "And your pursuit of property places you at the mercy of time, since within the constraints of this system, the adage 'time is money' is true. This situational complex corrupts your pursuit of happiness, turning your conscious perception of your life into bits and pieces."

Recalling our earlier conversations on happiness, I could not disagree.

"Albert Einstein said 'Reality is only an illusion, albeit a very persistent one.', but Albert was aware that time and matter or property are just sidetracks for the cosmic train. He was a master of the universe, not because he could do anything magical with his personal time or had a lot of money, but because he would not enslave himself to either."

"Easier said than done," I grumbled.

"True, even a Noble Savage has to deal with the basic constraints of life like finding food and housing." Homo sap agreed. "But, we do so in the context of the universe and life, not the artificial world of property and status. If we need to go hunting for food, we partner with time; we don't succumb to it. Do I wear a wristwatch?"

"No," I did not see one and never recalled him having one, but, of course, *he* was the savage; I thought to myself. (The designation of being a savage was starting to lose the derogatory tones I had previously attached to it. Somehow, if Homo Sap had called me a savage, I was wondering if I would perceive it as a badge of honor, of coming of age, on a cosmic level.)

"Where would he get one," I scoffed internally, but I knew that if Sap yearned for a timepiece he would have one. Heck, birds are well-known for picking up bright objects; if Homo Sap wanted one, he would have a top-of-the-line Rolex.

"Do you see me hoarding shells?"

I acknowledged with body language that I never saw him with any large accumulation of the shells, which the locals used as a form of currency.

"No," I admitted.

"Our shells are like civilized man's coins and paper, representing money," Homo Sap continued relentlessly. "But in the end, they are just shells, metal and paper. When one dies, the only thing you can take with you is the happiness you have generated in your life for you and the ones around you. For even the civilized man realizes that upon death, time and property cease to exist for the deceased."

"So we come back to the question," Homo Sap circled back. "Are you going to be a Homo sapiens or Homo sap? Do you want to focus the rest of your life upon the pursuit of time and property or happiness?"

I felt like the young man in the fairy tale given the choice between two doors, behind which were either a beautiful maiden or a hungry lion. And it was my turn to choose.

What would you do? What are you doing?

Epilogue

"Where is that good for nothing reporter? Where is my UFO article?" The tyrannical editor, Ed, muttered to himself as he walked down a tree-lined path. The reporter he was lambasting could have been Norman, but this is how Ed talked about all his reporters.

"UFO articles, I need UFO articles!" The tyrannical editor was talking to himself a lot nowadays. Then he looked around. "I got to make my doctor happy with these blasted walks to help my heart, but I have better things to do. Damn, it seems like birds have been chattering around me for days."

"He is a particularly stupid human, isn't he?"

"Who said that?" The tyrannical editor searched in every direction, but there were only a couple of ravens in a tree on his right.

"Who's there?"

The two ravens cocked their heads in different directions as they looked at Ed and Ed looked back. The first bird was larger with his black feathers rippling with a blue sheen in the sunlight. The second bird was smaller, but a little ruffled, as if he had just come from an unsuccessful hunt for food.

"Finally!"

Ed flinched as he realized that the words were emanating from the birds. After a short silence, Ed blurted "Birds can't talk."

"Then why are you talking with us?" the larger blue-black raven on the right said.

"This cannot be happening," Ed started muttering feverishly to himself. "I am losing my mind, hallucinating, or something."

"Not really," the smaller raven assured him. "We are bird-speaking; you remember Norman Rock's articles, don't you?"

"This can't be," Ed pleaded with the air about him.

"He is weird," the bigger bird said to the other. "Let's get this over with before something strange happens."

"Tyrannical Editor," the smaller raven spoke up. "All we want is for you to leave the window to your home office open today. It has to be left wide open, because we have a delivery for you."

"I have got to find a psychiatrist!" Ed wailed.

"If you don't open the window," the first, bigger, raven threatened. "We will come back and talk with you every day."

"Nice touch," the second, slighter, raven complimented the first.

"I'm going crazy!" Ed was starting to hyperventilate.

"Tut-tut," the first raven spoke sharply. "No such thing. You have heard of birds talking before, right? 'Polly want a cracker' stuff, right?"

"Well, Polly wants you to leave your office window open, that's all," the second raven turned his head to look at Ed, first, with one eye and then another. "Will you do this for us? If it will help, I can sound a little idiotic. How about 'Polly want window open!'?"

The bird used a rough voice, just like those huge parakeets used in the movies and followed this statement with a scratchy squawk. This comforted Ed quite a bit. If you must talk to a bird, the bird has to sound like a stupid bird. Ed's sensibilities would accept no more. (He was definitely civilized.)

"You want me to leave my window open?"

"He is a sharp one," the smaller raven observed.

"Yes," the larger raven replied in the scratchy voice, ignoring the smaller raven's sarcasm.

"OK, I can do that," Ed replied, somewhat in a daze. "Do you want me to leave you crackers?"

"No," the smaller raven replied quickly. "But a juicy squirrel carcass would be nice."

"Ignore him," the larger raven did not want to get sidetracked. "Just leave the window open today and we will be done. No crackers!"

"OK," the editor agreed.

"Thanks," the larger raven cocked his head at the editor and then both birds flew off.

To say the least, the editor arrived home in an agitated state. Talking to birds was not on his list of normal activities. This could only mean that something abnormal had occurred and being a control freak, the abnormal was most dismaying. Pacing around the house, he finally decided to leave the window open as requested. He called in sick (first time in 20 years) and hid. This must be a trick by some ventriloquist trying to burglarize his home, he rationalized, but in the back of his mind he was most afraid of the bird's threat to come back and talk with him the next day.

Ed situated himself in a chair just outside his office with the door open, so he could see everything. Nothing happened for hours. When he dozed off for a second, the fluttering of wings woke him up. Instantly, he looked in his office, but nothing was there except for a stack of manuscripts, Norman Rock's manuscripts, and a pile of digital cards packed with Perky's photos. A sticky-note was attached to the top document which said in Norman's handwriting: "Perky and I resign."

Ed tried to rationalize where all this new material had come from. He had not seen a bird; so someone must have sneaked in and played a practical joke on him. Birds don't talk and they don't deliver a box full of articles. While he was struggling with his lucidity, Ed started to sort through the manuscripts.

"You know, I think Norman was right; I do need a vacation," Ed was talking to himself, again, as he sifted through the pile, before he excitedly exclaimed. "A UFO article, I got my UFO article!"